Never Strikes Twice
Sunrise City 3

Never Strikes Twice
Sunrise City 3

By

Rodney Riesel

Published by Island Holiday Publishing

East Greenbush, NY

Special thanks to:

Pamela Guerriere

Kevin Cook

Cover Photo by:

Kim Seng at RoyalStockPhoto.com

Cover Design by:

Connie Fitsik

To learn about my other books friend me at

https://www.facebook.com/rodneyriesel

For Brenda,
Kayleigh, Ethan
& Peyton

Chapter One

Monday mornings suck. And this particular Monday morning was no different. Well, it was a little different, mainly because I was spending it sitting Indian-style on the floor of a convenience store. Why was I sitting on the floor of a convenience store? Because that's what you do when some shitbag walks in with a gun and yells, "Everybody on the floor!"

I sat with my back against the checkout counter; my fingers were laced together and resting in my lap. *Why did I have to stop for gas?* I thought. *I could have made it to work. And why didn't I just pay at the pump with my debit card?* Hind-sight is 20/20.

I wasn't the only one on the floor. There was a young mom and her son sitting to my right a few feet away from me, and a guy wearing a hard hat sat directly in front of me. A biker who had just gassed up his Harley was sitting to the construction worker's right. Hmm, a biker, a construction worker ... and I used to be a cop. If only one of the Village People were a young mom, we would be all set to go on tour. Yeah, that's the kind of things I think about while I devise a plan to beat the ever-living hell out of a shitbag.

I had been in hostage situations before—two that I could remember offhand—but I had never been the hostage. I glanced down at my wristwatch. It was 9:00 am. Leon, the cook, was probably the only person at Breakwater at this hour. I wish Leon were here now. He would probably walk up to that punk, slap the gun out of his hand, rip off his head, and shove it up his ass. I'll be the first to admit, I wasn't as brave as Leon—or as crazy, for that matter.

I put the palms of my hands on the floor to try and adjust my butt to a more comfortable position. My right hand skidded in something wet and sticky. I looked down. It was blood. Not my blood: the blood of the poor old guy who was working the register when Shitbag walked in. The old cashier tried to argue with the punk, and even reached for the punk's gun. The gun went off, by accident I think, and the old guy took one right between the eyes. It was his blood that was seeping under the counter next to me. And it was his brains all over the cigarette stand behind the counter.

The mom sat with her legs straight out in front of her. Her little boy lay on his side with his head resting on her lap. I gave them a *don't-worry-about-a-thing* smile. Neither smiled back. They were worried about everything.

The construction worker looked scared. He probably had a wife and kids, and was hoping to see them again soon. The biker was trying his best to look as though he wasn't scared of anything, not even death. I almost believed him.

The shitbag—a young white kid in his early twenties—stood with his back to us staring out the front plate-glass window at the Fort Pierce patrol car that had pulled up to get gas just as the gun went off. With his window down, the officer heard the shot, threw the unit in reverse, and backed up to the far side of the parking lot. He had called for backup which was sure to arrive any second now.

The punk's revolver hung at his side as he stared out the front window at the cop. He wore a white wife-beater and a pair of jeans that were at least three sizes too big for him. With his empty hand, he held the pants by the waistband.

"What's your name?" I asked.

The punk spun around and aimed the weapon at my face. "What?" he asked. His voice cracked. He was nervous. His face was covered in sweat.

"I asked your name."

"My name?"

"Yeah, that thing your mom calls you."

"I'm sure his mom calls him a lot of things," said the biker.

The punk swung the gun from me to the biker. "You better shut your mouth!"

The biker snickered. "Or what?"

He pulled back the revolver's hammer with his thumb. "Or the same thing will happen to you that happened to that old man," he said, pointing at the register. He tugged at his pants again.

"Ignore him," I said. "I'll just call you Bill."

He pointed the gun at me again. His eyes went to each of us sitting on the floor, and then he spun around and returned his attention to the cop outside. He put his hand on his head and said in a desperate undertone, "No no no!"

Three more units pulled up out front. There were probably a few in the back as well.

"The SWAT team will be here within five minutes," I said. "They'll take positions around the building. Every weapon will be trained on you through those great big windows."

"Shut up!" Bill hollered. He didn't turn around this time.

"Put down the weapon, Bill," I said, "and walk out the door slowly with your hands on your head."

He turned toward me. "What are you, a cop?"

"I used to be," I replied. "And trust me, this never ends well for punks named Bill."

I was with the Fort Pierce Police Department for twenty-five years. I retired a few years back and bought the Breakwater Bar and Grill. I hoped no one would ever point a gun at me again. We don't always get what we hope for.

I guess because the punk was concentrating on me, the biker figured that was his opportunity to make his heroic move. He leapt to his feet and made it about three steps. The punk was quicker than any of us thought. He turned the weapon and fired two rounds into the biker's chest. The biker's feet shot out from under him. I think he was probably dead before his back hit the cold tile floor.

The mom screamed and her son threw his arms around her. "Mommy!" he cried out.

"Shut up!" screamed Bill. He turned to me again. "Stand up!"

I started to climb to my feet.

"Sit down!" he hollered.

I froze. "Which is it, Bill? Stand up or sit down?"

"Sit down," he replied. He turned to the mom and her kid. "Get up."

She looked at me. Her eyes pleaded *help me*.

I went ahead and got to my feet to get a better look out the window. The SWAT van pulled up just as I looked.

The mom got to her feet; she pulled her little boy behind her. She was shaking.

"They're here," I said, trying my best not to sound like a poltergeist warning.

Bill looked over his shoulder and out the window as he crossed the floor to the mom.

"Time's running out," I said.

"Shut up! And sit down!" He grabbed the mom by the arm. "You're coming with me. We're getting out of here."

"Please, no," Mom begged.

"Mommy," said her little boy, "I'm scared.

"There's nowhere to go, Bill," I tried to convince him.

Bill stared down a hallway that ran between the beer coolers to a rear exit. "My car's out back."

I gave a derisive snort. "You don't think they're watching the back?" I glanced over at a can of Campbell's Chicken Noodle Soup on the checkout counter that the construction worker had placed there before the shit hit the fan. A scenario played out in my head wherein I picked up the soup can, threw it as hard as I could, hitting Bill in the head, and knocking him unconscious. *Soup cans are hard and heavy*, I thought. *Even if it didn't knock him out, it would stun him long enough for me to gain control of his weapon*. I looked Bill up and down. I could easily kick the shit out of him. Skinny little bastard.

"I told you to sit down," said Bill. He went for the door pulling, the woman with him.

She let go of her son. "Stay here, Timmy," she said.

The second Bill's back was turned, I grabbed Timmy with one hand and pointed at the front entrance with the other, telling the construction worker with my eyes to make a run for it; he did, and I ran with Timmy. I knew we only had seconds until Bill found the rear exit to be guarded. The construction worker grabbed Timmy by the other hand and the two of them scurried out the door. I could hear officers shouting "get on the ground" the second they were outside.

I turned around just as Bill pushed open the back door. Officers at the rear of the building began shouting orders at the punk; he fired his weapon twice out the back door, then yanked it shut. He let go of the woman and ran back into the store. The mom stayed by the exit door.

"Where's the kid!" Bill shouted. His world was falling apart before his eyes.

"He's outside," I said. I made eye contact with the mom. She turned, pushed open the door, and dashed out.

"Goddammit!" Bill shouted. He looked skyward. "Why, why!"

"Looks like it's just you and me, Bill" I said, "and you only got one bullet left."

Bill looked at the revolver in his hand.

The phone rang.

"You want me to get that, Bill?" I asked. "It's probably our friends outside."

"No. Yes."

"Make up your mind, Bill."

"Answer it."

I returned to the checkout counter and picked up the phone. "Circle K. Cole speaking. How may I help you?" I turned toward the front window, gave a big fake smile, and waved. I put my hand over the mouthpiece. "Smile for the cameras, Bill. The news is here."

"Who am I speaking with?" asked the caller.

"This is Cole Ballinger," I replied.

"Cole? It's Tommy Franklin."

"Hey, Tommy. What's up?" I put my hand over the phone again. "It's a friend of mine, Tommy Franklin," I told Bill. "He's a detective. Small world, huh?"

Bill didn't know what to say. I was starting to think this was Bill's first robbery. I was positive it was his first two murders, mainly because his face became a little grayer after each one. He looked as though he might puke up his Cap'n Crunch.

"How many others are in there?" Tommy asked.

"Just me and Bill," I replied. "Bill's the bad guy."

"Let me speak to him."

I held the phone out to Bill. "He wants to talk to you."

"Hang up," Bill ordered.

"Are you sure?" I asked.

"Put it on speaker."

I searched the keypad on the base and punched the speaker button. "You're on speaker, Tommy."

"This is Detective Tom—"

"I know who you are."

"Okay," Tommy replied. "Who am I speaking with?"

"Bill. Just Bill."

Huh. He likes the name Bill.

"Bill, let me know what we can do to end this."

Bill stood silent for a second, thinking. I knew he wasn't smart enough to come up with a plan. I almost felt bad for the piece of shit. I wondered if I should help him out.

"Tell them to bring your car around front," I whispered.

"Have someone bring my car around front!" Bill shouted. "It's the Chevy Nova out back. The keys are in it."

I grinned and nodded my head approvingly.

"We can do that," Franklin said.

Three minutes later the car was sitting out front, about fifteen yards from the door.

"They really should have parked it closer," I whispered.

"Move the car closer to the door!" Bill yelled.

"That's telling 'em," I said. "Cops. What are you gonna do?"

"Idiots," said Bill.

"We'll move it closer," said Franklin.

"Go to the door and tell the moron where exactly to park it," I said.

"Good idea," said Bill. He turned and started toward the door.

I turned and picked up the can of soup and threw it as hard as I could. It hit Bill in the back of the head with a cracking sound that made me a little nauseous. He stumbled forward two steps and crashed face first on the floor; his head bounced when he hit.

"Damn!" I said. "He's going to feel that when he wakes up."

I walked over to Bill and kicked his weapon to the other side of the store. I bent down and picked him up by the waistband of his baggy jeans and carried him out the front door. Blood dripped from his mouth, nose, and the back of his head, leaving a trail as I walked.

"Here you go, Tommy," I said. I dropped Bill in the middle of the parking lot. His face smacked the pavement. "Two bodies inside: an employee and some biker dude." I looked around the immediate area for the mom and her kid, or the construction worker. They were nowhere to be seen. I figured they were being looked over by a paramedic somewhere.

"What the hell did you do to him?" Tommy asked, when he got to me.

"Hit him in the head with a can of Campbell's soup."

"Tomato?"

"Chicken noodle."

"Never liked their chicken noodle soup. Always smelled like BO to me."

I looked down at Bill. "Yeah, it didn't seem to agree with him either."

I started walking toward the gas pumps where my truck still remained.

"Where are you going?" Tommy asked.

"Work," I replied.

"I'm going to need a statement."

I kept right on walking. "Stop down to the bar later. I'll give you a statement there."

"Why don't you just stop down to the station later?"

"I'll buy you lunch."

"I'll see you at the Breakwater around lunchtime."

Tommy Franklin never could pass up a free meal.

Chapter Two

It was a little after ten by the time I got to the Breakwater Bar and Grill. My adrenaline was still pumping from the gas station holdup. It's times like that that make me wonder why I ever retired. I was only two years older than Tommy Franklin. If he could still do it, so could I. I looked around the empty bar and dining room. *Oh, yeah*, I thought. *That's why I retired. For all this*. I shook my head and went into the kitchen.

"Mornin' boss," said Leon. He was at the grill, scraping it down with the back of a metal spatula.

"Morning, Leon," I responded.

Leon knew I had told him I would be in by nine and that I was an hour late, but he wouldn't say anything. He wouldn't even glance up at the clock, or stare at his arm at an imaginary wristwatch to bust my balls. I appreciated that about him, but at the same time it bugged me.

"I'm late," I said.

"Are ya?" Leon asked. "Hadn't noticed."

Yeah, right, I thought.

Leon had been with me almost since the opening of the Breakwater. As a matter of fact, I once shot him and sent him to jail for a few years. When he got out, he came looking for a job. What was I supposed to say, no? Hell, I had shot the guy. I couldn't turn him down for a job too. Besides, it was nice having a big guy like Leon around. He was six-three, a couple inches taller than me, and his biceps were as big around as my head. Sometimes I wondered if I hired him because I felt bad that I shot him, or because I was afraid that if I hadn't hired him that day, he would have come back later and killed me. Either way, it's worked out for the best, he's gotten me out of a few jams in the last couple years.

"You got the specials written down?" I asked. "I'll go put them on the chalkboard out front."

Leon pulled a wrinkled up napkin out of his back pocket and handed it to me. I opened the napkin and tried my best to make out the chicken scratch. Like most days, I wasn't even sure what it said. "Perfect," I said, and walked back to the bar scratching my head.

Just as I got back out front, Norma Winkle walked through the door. I handed her the napkin. "Can you write these specials on the board?"

She looked at the napkin. I watched her eyes as they moved across the words. "Sure," she said.

I wondered if she really knew what it said, or if she was just pretending.

Norma stepped behind the bar and pulled her apron out from underneath. She wrapped it around her waist and tied it in the front.

Norma had been with me from day one. She had worked for the last owner of the Breakwater, and after he sold the place to me, I asked her to stay on. I couldn't run the place without her. Norma was average height and thin. She had short brown hair with bangs that looked like they were cut by a chimp with an out-of-control weed-whacker. She had a long hook nose that reminded me of a predatory bird's beak. You know, one of those women who you look at and think, *that woman would be pretty if it wasn't for that schnoz*. Well, that wasn't Norma. A nose job from the best plastic surgeon in Hollywood wouldn't help that woman's looks.

"Who's on today?" I asked.

"Allison and me for lunch," Norma replied. "And Emily comes in at three."

Allison, twenty-two, is my oldest daughter; she's been working at the Breakwater for about a year. She's a good kid.

"Did you bring the morning newspaper?" I asked.

Norma was writing the specials on the chalkboard. "No, sorry, Cole. I didn't stop and grab one on my way in this morning."

I walked to the entrance door and stared out the glass at Jetty Park while pondering my next move. *Should I just go in and use the toilet with no reading material, or should I walk up to the corner of Ocean Drive and get one out of the stand?* It was a tough decision to make. *I could read my cell phone.* I reached into my pocket and checked for change. "Norma, grab me a few quarters out of the register."

"Sure, Cole. I'm not doing anything," she said with heavy sarcasm.

"Never mind."

"No," she said. "I got it."

With my quarters in hand, I walked up the street toward the newspaper stand. About halfway there, my stomach began to gurgle. I looked back over my shoulder at the Breakwater, then back at the newspaper stand. I decided to keep going. I picked up my pace. I had the first quarter readied between my thumb and index finger. I was a man on a mission.

I was almost there when I heard, "Hey, Cole, can I speak to you for a second."

Shit! I turned around. It was Herb Bean, the owner of the Jetty Lounge. He was walking through his parking lot toward me.

"I haven't got time right now, Herb," I said. I think my voice cracked a little. I kept moving toward the newspaper box. I stuck my four quarters in and pulled open the door. It slipped from my fingertips and slammed shut. I yanked on the door. It had relocked and wouldn't budge. "Dammit!"

"Cole," Herb said.

"Not now, Herb," I responded. "Wait. Herb, you got some change for the paper?"

Herb reached into his front pocket and pulled out a nickel, three pennies, and a dime. "Sorry."

I felt beads of sweat forming on my forehead.

A car pulled to the curb and a guy got out. He walked up to the yellow metal box. I stepped back. He put in his change and pulled out his newspaper.

"Let me grab one of those," I said.

The guy gave me a disgusted look. "That's stealing," he informed me.

"Cole," said Herb. "It'll only take a second."

"Not now, Herb. Jesus Christ!"

I grabbed the door and the guy tried to force it shut. "Listen, asshole," I said. "I need that newspaper, and I ain't got time to explain." My stomach gurgled again, and it felt like Mr. Poop knocking at my sphincter.

He managed to force the door closed. I heard the lock click.

"You bastard!" I shouted. I grabbed the guy's newspaper out of his hand and made a run for it.

I could hear the guy hollering "Come back here!" as I entered the Breakwater. I ran through the bar, down the hall, and into the men's room. I yanked down my cargo shorts and sat. I let out a big sigh, and opened the paper. KIM KARDASHIAN MAKES A BIG SPLASH ON THE RED CARPET the headline on the Arts and Entertainment section read. *Big deal,* I thought. *I did that right here in the men's room.* I chuckled quietly at my own joke.

When I returned to the bar with the newspaper tucked into my armpit, Norma and my new friend from the newspaper stand were waiting for me.

"This man says you stole his paper?" Norma declared, in the form of a question.

"I didn't steal it, I borrowed it," I explained. I held it out to the guy. "Here you go. You can have it back."

"I don't want it back now," said the guy disgustedly. "You had it in the bathroom."

I shrugged and tossed the paper on the bar. "It's there when you change your mind," I said.

"Really, Cole?" Norma asked. She went to the register, counted out a dollar in quarters, and handed them to the guy. "Here," she said. "Sorry for any inconvenience. Stop back down some time—lunch is on us."

He took the quarters, said thanks, and left. But not before giving me another dirty look.

"You want me to buy that jerk a meal?" I asked.

"So, he was the jerk?" Norma asked.

"Pretty much." I saw the beer truck pull up out front and craned my neck, but the glare on the windshield prevented me from seeing who was driving. I turned and started for the kitchen. Halfway to the kitchen door, I paused and turned around. "Hey, Norma."

"Yeah?"

"The headline in the paper said Kim Kardashian makes a big splash on the red carpet …"

"And?"

I stood there for a second silently staring at her. "Never mind." I walked through the kitchen door just as the beer guy pushed his handcart through the rear entrance.

"Morning, Mr. Ballinger," said the delivery guy.

"Morning, Ed," I replied.

The new beer guy was Ed Castillo; he was twenty-four. I had told him several times to call me Cole, but every time he came through the door, it was "Morning, Mr. Ballinger." I could never tell if he was being polite or just wanted to make me feel old. Ed had been delivering my beer for eight weeks now; he was Kelly Morgan's replacement while Kelly was on the mend from injuries he sustained in an altercation weeks ago.

Besides being my usual beer delivery guy, Kelly was a good friend of mine. I guess you could say with my short list of friends, he's probably my best friend. I'm probably his best friend as well, but that fact is an unspoken aspect of our relationship, mainly because if I told him he was my best friend, he would think I was hitting on him. Kelly's the most homophobic man I've ever met in my life.

"Good morning, Leon," said Ed.

"Morning, Ed."

I wondered if Ed knew that Leon was four years older than me. I watched him wiggle his hand truck out from under the cases of beer. He returned to his truck for more while I put the ones he brought in into the walk-in cooler.

After the beer had been delivered and put away, I returned to the bar. I glanced up at the wall clock that hung just below the plastic marlin on the wall across from the bar; it was almost eleven. Allison was supposed to be in at ten.

Allison was a pretty good worker, even though she was always late. Her work ethic wasn't really the reason I liked her working at the Breakwater. It was because I enjoyed spending time with her at work. It made everyday kind of like a father/daughter project. I didn't get to spend a lot of time with her and her brother and sister, because her mother and I divorced when they were little. I got them every other weekend for a few hours while they were growing up. Between their mother's wrath and my work schedule, that was about all I could manage. I figured letting Allison work here was my way of making up for lost time. I figured I would probably do the same thing for CJ when he was old enough to work here. Would I someday let Angel work at the bar? Probably not, but that's another story.

When Norma left the room, I grabbed the napkin off the bar and walked over by the specials board. I compared what Norma had written with what Leon had written on the napkin. *Wow*, I thought. *That's what that said?*

The door opened and in walked Allison. "I know, I know," she said. "I'm late."

"Hadn't noticed," I replied.

"I spent the night at Spence's place last night and—"

I put my hands over my ears. "Na-na-na-na-na," I said. "Don't want to hear about you staying at Spence's."

Allison stared at me until I put my hands down. "I wasn't going to say anything inappropriate," she let me know. She reached under the bar and grabbed her apron.

Spence, was Detective Spence Oller. He and Allison had been dating for almost six months. Spence was seven years older than Allison, but I didn't fight the relationship because Spence is a really great guy. The perfect guy, as a matter of fact, for any man's daughter. Spence was polite, responsible, and the only swear word I had ever heard him say was hell ... and that was only once.

Allison jumped behind the bar and tied her apron around her waist. "What do you want me to do first?" she asked.

"The same thing you did first yesterday," I replied.

She untied her apron, tossed it back under the bar, and headed to the kitchen for the mop and bucket. When she was almost to the door she turned around. "Oh, yeah—uh, Dad?" she asked.

"How much?" I asked.

She cocked her head. "What makes you think I was going to ask for money?"

"Your tone."

"Oh. Well, can I borrow twenty? I'm on E."

"Sure." I pulled out my wallet and pulled out a twenty. "Am I going to get this back?"

Allison walked over and snatched the money out of my hand. "I could say yes ... but we would both know I was lying."

"At least you're honest."

She got up on her tip-toes and kissed me on the cheek. "Love ya." She smiled big showing the million dollar teeth it took me six years to pay off.

"You better," I replied.

She turned and went for the mop.

The entrance door opened. "Cole, can I speak to you for a second?"

It was Herb Bean again.

I sighed loudly. I hoped it was loud enough to let Herb know that I had no interest in listening to what he had to say. I knew it was probably something about kids throwing shit in his dumpster or someone from my place blocking his parking spot. Herb was a nice guy, as far as people I have no use for go. Herb was short, about five feet four. His jet black hair was in the shape of a horseshoe that ran from one temple, around the back of his head, and to the other temple. He was completely bald on top. More times than not, Herb had a Band-Aid covering some small injury on top of his bald dome. I don't know what it was that he kept running his head into over the years, but you'd think by now he would have learned his lesson.

Most men Herb's size usually wore shorts that were too long for them, but Herb's shorts were always three or four inches above his knee, leading me to guess that he purchased them from Baby Gap. He was also the only man

I knew who still wore tube socks; and what made it even worse, he wore them with his sandals.

"What is it this time, Herb?" I asked. My eyes went to the wall clock just to let him know that he was being timed, and I was being impatient.

"Can we talk in private?" Herb asked.

I scanned the empty room. "We're the only ones here, Herb."

Herb pointed at the door that led out to the beach. "Can we step outside?"

"You're not going to kick my ass, are you?"

Herb looked surprised by the question. "Goodness, no," he replied.

"I know, Herb. I was joking."

"Oh. Good one, Cole."

I started toward the door and Herb followed. We walked out the door, past the picnic tables and bandstand, and around the volleyball net to the beach.

Herb stood with his hands in his pockets, staring out toward the jetty. It was obvious by the look in his eye that something was troubling him deeply. I waited for him to start talking. I didn't wait long.

"What's the matter, Herb?" I finally asked.

"It's my wife," he replied. His voice cracked a little when he said wife.

I didn't really know Herb's wife, Bambi. I had seen her around and run into her a few times out front when arriving at my place, or saw her getting out of her Audi when I was driving by. I don't even remember ever speaking to her. Our only interaction was the nod of the head or maybe one of those uncomfortable *hi there* smiles. I do remember on a few occasions thinking, W*ow, she is way too hot for Herb.* Bambi was tall, thin, and blonde with after-market boobs and lips. I had always assumed the upgrades were purchased by Herb.

"What about your wife?" I asked.

"She didn't come home last night," said Herb.

"Okay. And?"

"She didn't come home the night before either."

"How about the night before that?"

"She was home Friday night."

"When was the last time you saw her, Herb?"

"Saturday evening around six o'clock."

"What happened at six?"

"She said she was running to Publix to get groceries."

"Which Publix?"

"I'm not sure."

"Have you contacted the police?"

"No."

"You haven't heard from her at all?"

"No."

"You haven't seen or heard from your wife in two days and you haven't notified the police. Why?"

"I was afraid they would think I had done something wrong."

"Something like what, Herb?"

"Like I killed her or something."

"Why would they think you killed your wife?"

"Because every time a woman disappears, the cops—and Nancy Grace—automatically think the husband killed her."

"Well, that's because most of the time it is the husband. *Did* you have anything to do with Bambi's disappearance?"

Herb rolled his eyes and threw back his head. "See what I mean?"

"I'm not accusing you! I'm just asking a question."

"I didn't have anything to do with her disappearance. I swear to God."

Well, he had sworn to God, so he was pretty much innocent. If I had a dime for every time I heard some piece of shit say, "I didn't do it. I swear to God—well, I guess I would have about a hundred bucks in change."

"So, are you going to help me?" Herb asked.

"I think you should just call the police, and let them handle it."

"You know what will happen, Cole. I'll report her missing, and they'll immediately focus their entire investigation on me."

"Investigation? What investigation? They'll put out a missing person—"

"And when she doesn't show up, they'll turn their attention to me."

"Why are you so sure she isn't going to turn up?"

"Do they ever turn up?"

"Yes. Most times missing people are found." *Wow*, I thought. *Someone has been watching far too many episodes of* Forensic Files.

"Sorry, Cole, but I'm just not that optimistic. I'm begging you. Are you going to help me?"

He wasn't begging, he wasn't even on his knees, but there was something about Bambi's disappearance that intrigued me. Why wasn't Herb very upset? Why did he wait two days? Why was he so sure he would never see his wife again, and why was he so sure he would be blamed?

"Fine," I said. "I'll look into it."

"Thank you."

"What time can I stop over to your house today?"

"Why do you need to come to my house?"

"I want to have a look around."

"Why?"

"Listen, Herb, if you want me to do this, we're going to do it my way and you're not going to question me the entire time. Got it?"

"Got it."

"What time can I stop over?"

"Seven o'clock tonight be okay?"

"That would be good."

I gave Herb my cell phone number and told him to text me his address. He left and I walked back inside the bar. When I got inside, Leon, Norma, and Allison were all standing around the bar staring at the television; their backs were to me.

"No one has anything to do?" I asked.

Allison turned and pointed at the TV. "Holy crap, Dad, you were at the Circle K this morning when it was held up?"

"Oh, yeah. I forgot to tell you about that." I caught a glimpse of myself in the footage, *I could stand to knock off a few pounds*, I thought, *but I still look pretty damn good*. I sucked in my belly.

"Two people were murdered," Allison pressed.

"Yup."

"Are you okay?"

"I'm fine."

Leon turned with a big grin. "You knocked the guy out with a can of soup?"

"Yup."

"Tomato?"

"Chicken noodle."

"Huh. Chicken noodle. Imagine that."

"They're calling you a hero," said Norma.

"Good," I said. "Maybe business will pick up around here. Who wouldn't want to eat at the restaurant of a hero?"

Allison came over and put her arms around me. "We could have lost you."

"Nonsense," I replied. "The bullets would have bounced off my chest."

Norma picked up the remote and flipped the TV to another station. They were talking about me on that channel too.

"Wow," Norma said. "You've made quite a splash on local television."

"That's nothing," I said. "You should have seen the splash I made in the bathroom earlier."

Allison pulled away and looked up at me. She had a disgusted look on her face. Norma and Leon both turned toward me and stared. No one laughed. They all just shook their heads and returned to work.

How is that not funny? I thought.

Chapter Three

It was a few minutes after noon when Melvin Mulhern hobbled through the door. "Saw ya on the old boob tube this morning," he said.

"Yup," I replied.

"They say you're pretty quick with a can of soup."

"Fastest can in the South," I said.

Melvin boarded his favorite barstool and reached into his pocket for the Ziploc sandwich bag in which he kept his money. He pulled open the top, reached inside, and plucked out a twenty. He tossed the bill on the bar; I set a rocks glass full of Scotch with a lemon twist next to it.

"Tomato?" he asked.

"Chicken noodle," I answered. I took his twenty and gave him back his change.

Melvin was about a million years old and one of my regulars. He was a regular when the last guy owned the place as well, and probably the guy before that. I often mused that Melvin had just crawled out of the ocean on all fours, lost his tail, and made one of the barstools his home. Melvin showed up most weekdays between eleven and one with a grumpy look on his face. Sometimes he would have lunch and sometimes not. He would usually stay for around three or four hours, have two drinks and then leave.

A man and woman in their late forties walked in. I pointed toward the dining room. "You can sit anywhere you like," I told them. "Someone will be right over."

"Thanks," the woman said. They went into the dining room and settled at one of the six four-tops.

I looked around, there was no waitress in sight. I took my cell phone out of my pocket and dialed the Breakwater's phone number. After six rings Norma answered.

"Breakwater Bar and Grill," said Norma. "How may I help you?"

"Yeah, I was wondering if I could get a waitress to take an order, please?" I asked.

"Cole, is that you?"

"Yup."

"Why are you calling here?"

"Because I need a waitress to get an order from the couple that just came in."

"You're a jackass." *Click!*

Norma walked through the kitchen door seconds later and went to the table. "How are you folks today?" she asked. She gave me a dirty look.

After Norma took their order, she came to the bar. "Two Mic Ultras," she said.

I grabbed the beers and set them on the bar. "There ya go." I gave her a big smile.

"Don't do that again," she warned, "or next time I'll put that phone where the sun don't shine."

I looked over at Melvin. He laughed, I didn't. I knew Norma wasn't joking. She picked up the beers and returned to her table.

The entrance door opened again. A table of four walked in, then another table of two. The next time the door opened, it was Detective Spence Oller, Allison's boyfriend. Spence was tall, in good shape, with his short hair parted on the side. He wore a suit and looked more like a TV version of an FBI agent than he did a Fort Pierce police detective. He smiled at me, revealing his perfect teeth. If I didn't know better, I would swear he was switched at birth, and the real Spence Oller was now living with the Osmond family.

"Just the man I wanted to see," I said.

The smile left his face. "Oh yeah?" he asked. "Why is that? You're not going to hit me with a can of tomato soup are you?"

Melvin burst out laughing again. Some of his biggest laughs are at my expense. Melvin's shoulders shook and he could hardly catch his breath during one of his laughing spells. Spence and I both looked over at him. As usual, his face was turning blue. Melvin always turned blue during a good laugh. Everyone stopped what they were doing and watched and waited for him to die, but he always pulled through. He took a deep breath and the normal pale color returned to his face. Everyone went back to what they were doing.

"It was chicken noodle soup," I informed him. "I need you to run a background check on a couple of people for me—a husband and wife."

"Why me? Why can't you ask your good buddy Tommy Franklin to do it for you?"

"Because Tommy Franklin's not dating my daughter."

Spence pulled a pad and pen out of the inside pocket of his jacket. "What are their names?" he asked defeatedly.

"Herb and Bambi Bean," I said.

"Bambi Bean? She a stripper?"

"Not that I know of. Why?"

"May I call your attention to the center stage," Spence announced, in his best ringmaster voice, "and the beautiful Miss Bambi Bean."

Spence had probably never been in a strip bar in his life, but if he had, I don't know which one, because my attention had never been directed to a center stage. I just shrugged.

"You got an address on them?"

I pulled out my cell and tapped the screen. Still no text from Herb. "Not yet." I tossed the phone onto the back bar next to the cash register.

"You don't know where they live?"

"Not really."

"Do they live here in Fort Pierce?"

"I think so."

Spence flipped his notepad shut and stuck it back in his pocket. "I figure you're not going to tell me why I'm looking at these two."

"You're turning into a great detective, Spence."

Spence sat down on a bar stool two down from Melvin and nodded at the old man. "Hey, Melvin," he said.

"Spence," Melvin replied.

"What can I get you to drink, Spence?" I asked.

"Ginger ale," he responded.

I already knew it was ginger ale before he answered. Spence doesn't really drink alcohol that much, and he sure wouldn't do it while on duty. I poured his soda and slid it across the bar just as Allison walked into the room.

"Hi, honeybun," said Allison.

Spence's face turned red.

Melvin glanced over with a surprised look. "Honeybun?" he asked.

Allison put her arms around Spence's neck and kissed him on the cheek. "He's my honeybun."

"Detective Honeybun," Melvin mumbled. "Ain't that sweet."

"I asked you not to call me that in front of other people," Spence scolded.

"These aren't other people," Allison replied. "It's just my dad and Melvin."

"Exactly. The two guys who will never let me live it down."

"Don't worry, Detective Honeybun," I said. "We won't say a word. Will we, Melvin?"

"Heavens no," said Melvin.

"I just had two tables sit down," Allison told Spence. "So I won't be able to go to lunch today."

"That's fine," said Spence.

"Do you want me to have Leon fix you something?"

"Yes, that would be great. How about a cheeseburger and fries?"

"Coming right up." Allison spun on her heels and headed for the kitchen.

My cell phone rang and I patted my pocket in search of it. I turned and picked it up off the back bar. I didn't recognize the number. "Hello?"

"Daddy?"

"Angel?" I stepped away from the bar to be out of earshot.

"Yes."

Angel was my middle child; she had been out of rehab for about seven weeks. I hadn't seen her in a week, and I knew that was a bad sign. It was also a bad sign the last four times she got out of rehab. The day she got out, she said she was going to turn her life around. She was done with drugs and she wanted to start college. She told us all that she was sorry for what she had put us through over the past several years. She told us she couldn't believe what she had done to herself, and that today was the start of a new life. It was a great speech. It was a great speech that day, just like it was a great speech all the other times she gave it. If you could call a story full of clichés and empty promises great

"Who's phone are you using?" I asked.

"A guy I know," she replied.

"Where's the phone I got you?"

"It's around here somewhere." Angel's speech was slow and deliberate; she was trying to enunciate every syllable in an attempt to sound sober. It didn't work. I knew she was either drunk or had smoked or shot up something.

"Where are you?"

"At a friend's house."

"That friend have a name?"

"Why, so you can do a background check on him?"

"No, I'm just a little worried. I haven't seen you in a few days."

"I'm fine. I was just calling to, uh … see if I could borrow a few dollars."

"Angel, you know I'm not going to give you any money. Your mother and I decided—"

"Mom gave me money yesterday."

"Well, she shouldn't have."

"I just need some money for food. I haven't eaten all day."

"What did you do with the money your mother gave you?"

"I owed it to somebody."

"For drugs?"

"Daddy, can I borrow the money or not?"

It was hard to say no, but I knew I had to. I had been a cop for long time and had seen a lot of parents go through this. I knew how it was probably going to end, but I was not going to pay for whatever she was putting into her veins or her lungs.

"No," I said.

"Why? Don't you love me? I have no food."

"I'm not giving you any money, Angel. If you want to come by the restaurant, I'll have Leon make you something to eat."

"I fucking hate you!" she screamed.

I said nothing. I couldn't have said anything if I wanted to. It was hard to speak with a knife in your heart that was being twisted by one of your own children.

"Remember, I know what you did," she threatened. "I know you killed Ted Hale. I can go to the cops at any time. I'll tell them everything. Everyone thinks you're such a great person. I know things—"

"I'm going to hang up, Angel."

"You're piece of shit!" she yelled. "I'll tell them every—"

I hung up and slipped my phone into my front pocket.

"Everything okay?" Spence asked.

"Everything's fine," I replied.

Chapter Four

It was two o'clock by the time Herb Bean text messaged me his address, and I relayed that message onto Spence.

Melvin slid off his barstool and started for the door. "I better get going," he said. "I want to get a nap in before bedtime."

I chuckled. "You take care of yourself, Melvin."

"Already took care of myself this morning," he replied. "Been taking care of myself ever since the last girlfriend took off."

"Gross," said Allison, who was walking out of the dining room.

Melvin's head spun around. "Oops," he said. "You weren't supposed to hear that, princess." He walked out the door and headed across Jetty Park to his old Buick.

"I need two Coronas, Daddy," said Allison, on her way to the kitchen.

"Coming right up," I said. I grabbed the two bottles out of the cooler behind me and popped off the tops. I jammed a lime wedge into each bottle, and slid them toward the edge of the bar.

I glanced up at the wall clock. Still five hours until I had to be at Herb's place. I wished I had something else to do until then. Kelly Morgan usually stopped by on Monday afternoons between two-thirty and three, when he got out of work. His visits always helped to break up the boredom of a long slow Monday. *Maybe I should give him a call*, I thought. I grabbed my cell phone off the back bar and dialed his number.

"Hello?" Kelly answered.

"Hey, what's going on?" I asked.

"Not much," he replied. "Just sitting here watching Dr. Oz."

I picked up the remote control and flipped the channel over to NBC. "Yeah? What's he talking about?"

"I don't know. Something about a root or a vegetable or something that's supposed to make people shit better."

"Huh, what's it called?" I stared at the television.

"Don't remember."

"Oh well, maybe next he'll talk about a berry that improves your memory so you can remember the name of the root that helps you shit."

"Only in a perfect world, my friend. Hey, I saw you on the TV this morning."

"Yeah, I'm famous."

"Said you hit a guy in the head with a bowl of soup, or something."

"It was a can of soup."

"Chicken noodle?"

"Yes! Thank you. Everyone else thought it would be tomato for some reason."

"Tomato soup is heavier, I guess."

"Yeah, that makes sense. You going to stop down here today for a drink?"

"Miss me?"

"No."

"My neurologist hasn't cleared me to drive yet, but I have an appointment with my primary tomorrow morning at ten."

"They say when you can get back to work?"

"They're saying four to six weeks yet."

"How're the headaches?"

"Haven't had a headache in over two weeks."

"That nurse still stopping by to … *take care of you*?"

"Um, no."

"Didn't work out?"

"Well, yes and no," Kelly replied. "I really liked her. She came over a few times; spent the night once. Everything seemed to be going great. Then her husband found out, and that was the end of that."

"Husband? Did you know she had a husband?"

"Not till he called me."

"Holy shit. How did he get your number?"

"He got it off her phone."

"Wow."

"Yeah. So anyway, that's that."

"And Bob's your uncle."

"Exactly."

"So, do you need anything?"

"I need a ride to the doctor tomorrow morning."

"Ten?"

"Pick me up at nine."

"You got it. See ya then."

I hung up the phone and tossed it on the back bar next to the cash register. I checked the wall clock again. Ugh! The day was dragging by.

The door opened and in walked Detective Tommy Franklin and his wonderful new partner, Detective Dan Kind.

"What's up, gentlemen?" I asked.

"Same shit, different odor," Tommy answered.

"Hey, Cole," said Kind.

I gave him a nod. He and Tommy took seats at the bar with one stool between them—you know, so they wouldn't look like lovers.

"Can I get you something to drink?" I asked.

Tommy looked around the room to make sure no one was close by. "Put a Jack and Coke in a soda cup," he said. "It's been a long day."

"I'll just have a coffee, if ya got it," Kind said.

I poured Tommy's Jack Daniels into a plastic tumbler full of ice and then added a little Coke. Then I jabbed a bendy straw into the cup to complete the illusion. "Here ya go," I said as I slid it across the bar.

Allison walked through the kitchen door. "Allison," I said. "Can you get Detective Kind a cup of coffee, please?"

"Sure," she said with a smile. She spun on her heels and returned to the kitchen.

"Cream or sugar?" I asked.

"Just black," Kind said.

I poured myself a half cup of soda with no ice, took a sip, placed it on the bar, and leaned back against the back bar. I folded my arms over my chest and crossed my legs. "So, what brings you gentlemen in today?" I knew what brought them in, but I asked anyway.

Tommy sipped his drink through the bendy straw.

"Just wanted to ask you a few questions about the incident this morning, Cole," Kind explained.

Tommy shot him a look. "He knows why we're here."

Kind shrugged.

Allison came through the door with Kind's coffee. "Here you go, sir," she said, placing the steaming mug in front of him.

"Call me Dan," Kind requested. He gave Allison a big stupid grin.

"Okay," Allison replied.

"You're Cole's daughter?" Kind asked.

"Yes," said Allison.

"She's Spence Oller's girlfriend," Tommy threw in.

Kind stuck out his hand. "It's nice to meet you," he said. "Spence is a great guy. We went through the academy together. Tell him I asked about him."

"I'll do that," Allison said. She turned to me. "Daddy, I'm taking off."

"Okay, princess."

She walked around the bar and gave me a kiss on the cheek. "Love you."

"Love you too," I said. She turned and left.

"So, you were just getting gas this morning, Cole?" Tommy asked.

"Yeah."

"Why did you go there?" Kind asked. "It's a little out of your way isn't it?"

"This is going to sound crazy," I said. I leaned in a little closer. "But I had a dream last night that there was going to be a robbery there at that Circle K this morning."

Kind's eyes widened. "Are you shittin' me?"

Tommy and I busted out laughing. "Yeah, I'm shittin' you! I go there because it's one of the last places around that you don't have to pay before you pump."

"Bastards," Kind said, shaking his head.

"How long were you in there before Josh—that's the kid's name—came in?" Tommy asked.

"Huh, I liked the name Bill better." Kind's vacant stare indicated an explanation was in order, but I was in no mood. "Maybe two minutes," I said. "The biker was over by the coffee maker, the woman and her kid were to my left, in the candy aisle, the contractor was standing at the counter in front of me. I think he had a cup of coffee in one hand and he had just set the can of soup down on the counter. The kid came in and screamed, 'Nobody move!'".

"Nobody move," Tommy repeated. "Original."

I continued. "He waved his weapon around and when it was pointed at the old guy behind the register, it went off. I don't think he meant to shoot the guy."

"What about the biker?" "Oh, he meant to shoot the biker."

I spent the next few minutes giving Tommy and Kind a detailed account of my heroism, ending with my Hail Mary of the soup can. When I finished, Kind said, "The old man's name was Cliff Sanders. He was Josh's grandfather."

I looked at Tommy. "Seriously?"

Tommy shook his head yes.

"The kid wasn't wearing a mask," I pointed out.

"We think the old man was probably in on it."

"He didn't look too broken up about shooting Gramps."

"He was pretty broken up in the ambulance on the way to the hospital when he told us."

"But he didn't admit to Gramps being in on the robbery?"

"No. He says it was all him."

"You believe him?"

"No, but we'll question him some more when he wakes up."

"Wakes up?" I asked.

"He lost consciousness again right after he spoke with us."

"Hasn't woke up since," Kind added.

"Geeze, I didn't think I hit him that hard."

"The doc said you hit him hard enough to crack his skull," said Tommy. "There was even some swelling and bleeding."

"Cerebral edema and subdural hematoma," offered Kind.

We both gave him a look.

"No one likes a smartass," said Tommy.

"The old man have a wife?" I asked.

"No," said Kind. "And the kid's mother, Wanda, was Cliff's only child."

"She died two months ago … cancer," Tommy added.

"The kid have any siblings?" I asked.

"A sister," Kind answered. "Her name's Lacey; same last name as the old man."

"But we haven't located her," said Tommy.

"How old?"

"Seventeen," said Kind.

I shook my head. "Poor kid," I said. "She's lost her entire family in the last two months."

Tommy took one last suck on his straw and the loud gurgling sound told everyone that the cup was empty. He slid it back across the bar. "I could go for about four more of those," he said. He climbed off his stool. "Come on, Kind, let's hit the road."

Tommy and Kind left, without paying for their drinks, I might add. I looked at the clock again and sighed loudly.

Norma exited the kitchen. "Can you have Leon make me a BLT?" I asked.

"Yes, your highness," she said. "Would you like chips or fries with that?"

"No, thanks. Just the sandwich."

Norma bowed two or three times as she backed through the kitchen door. I knew she was just being a wiseass, but at the same time, I enjoyed her show of respect. After all, I was a hero who had thwarted an armed robbery using nothing more than a can of chicken noodle soup. I turned and stared out the window across Jetty Park with my fists on my hips. If only I was wearing a cape and a large fan was blowing on me, the scene would be complete.

Chapter Five

I pulled into Herb and Bambi Bean's driveway around 6:45. I was fifteen minutes early, but I wanted to get this over with.

Herb and Bambi lived in three-story home on Watersong Way in Fort Pierce. The four bedroom, four bath home had a white steel roof with wooden clapboard siding, painted robin's egg blue. Watersong was a relatively new housing development located right on the beach. It consisted of one street—Watersong Way—that could only be accessed from a gate on South Ocean Drive. A four-by-eight billboard near the gate said, LOTS AVAILABLE. STARTING AT $499,000. So far only about ten houses had been built.

I parked in the brick horseshoe driveway and got out of my truck. I turned and looked out over the ocean. I was squinting even behind my aviators. I reached back into my truck, grabbed a small notepad off the dashboard, and slammed the door. I looked up at Herb's house as I shoved the notepad into my back pocket. *Wow*, I thought. *My restaurant is bigger than his. Why does he live in this McMansion, and I have to live in a two-bedroom apartment? Shit! I wish I had a pen or pencil.*

I walked up the steps to the second floor, which was the main floor of the home. From the looks of it, the entire first floor was a two-stall garage. I rang the doorbell and then rapped on the door a few times with my knuckles. A second or two later Herb pulled open one of the large double doors.

"You're early," He said.

"I thought I might catch you in the backyard digging a big hole," I replied.

"What?"

"Just kidding, Herb. Can I come in?"

"Of course."

Herb stepped back from the door and I went in. He shut the door behind me. I smelled a strong lemony odor right away.

"Been cleaning house, Herb?" I asked.

"Yeah. Why?" he replied.

"Because I can smell it." As Herb led me down the hall I glanced into the living room. There was an empty bottle of wine on a glass coffee table, and next to it was an empty wine glass.

"I just made coffee. Would you like a cup?" Herb asked.

"Sure," I said.

We walked into the kitchen. To our left was the dining room. The two rooms were separated only by an island. A glass door was directly in front of me and over-looked the pool and sunken hot tub in the backyard.

Herb grabbed two mugs out of a cabinet above the coffeemaker and placed them on the countertop.

"Cream or sugar?" he asked.

"Black," I said.

He poured each cup and handed me mine. He didn't add cream or sugar to his either, but when he sipped it, his cringe told me he probably didn't usually drink his black. I wondered if he was trying to impress me by not adding the sweeteners. He seemed like that type of guy. I figured he only swore if he was around other men who swore, and only talked sports for the same reason. I've known a lot of nerdy guys who would try to blend in with men they thought were cool or manly. They never fooled anyone but themselves.

"Where do you want to start?" Herb asked.

I took a gulp of my coffee. It was hotter than shit and I burned my tongue, but I didn't flinch. I wouldn't want to spoil Herb's manly man image of me. "Why were you cleaning?" I asked.

Herb looked at me like I was nuts and should already know the answer to that. "I always do my housework on Monday," he said.

"Oh," I replied. "And what day does Bambi do her housework?"

"Bambi doesn't do house work. We have a housekeeper who comes every other Wednesday, and I do it on Mondays."

"Hmm," I said nodding. "I've been looking for a housekeeper."

"Would you like our lady's phone number?"

"No, Herb, I was hoping I could hire you to do it."

"Me?" he asked.

"I'm kidding, Herb."

"Oh. Good one, Cole."

"Yeah, I'm funny as shit." I turned and started back down the hall. "Let's head upstairs."

"Why do you want to go up there?"

"To have a look around."

Herb shrugged. "Okay."

I walked up the stairs first and he followed. The bathroom was at the top of the stairs. I pushed the door open and looked inside. It was spotless. Herb was a great maid.

"That's the bathroom," said Herb.

"Yeah, the toilet gave it away."

I backed up and bumped into Herb. I gave him a look.

"Sorry, Cole."

I pushed open the next door I came to.

"Bedroom," Herb said.

"Yeah." There was a full size bed two dressers, and an en suite bathroom.

"A guest room," said Herb.

"Who was the last guest?"

"We've never had a guest."

"Well, at least you're prepared."

"We've only lived here for about eight months."

"You know any of your neighbors?"

"Not really. Just to wave if one drives by."

"Do they wave back?"

"Yes. Why wouldn't they?"

"I don't know." The next door I came to was another bedroom. It was the same size as the first and decorated pretty much in the same manner. "Another guest room?" I asked.

"Yes."

The third door was locked. "What's in here?" I asked.

"Another bedroom," Herb replied.

"Why is it locked?"

"I don't know."

"What do you mean, you don't know?"

"I mean … Bambi always kept it locked."

"Does she go in there?"

"Yes … I guess."

"Have you ever been in there?"

"Of course."

"Get the key."

"I would have to look for it."

"Never mind." I side stepped to the next door and opened it. It was the master bedroom. I went in.

"This where the magic happens?" I asked.

"Magic?" Herb asked.

"Sex, Herb. I was talking about sex."

"Oh."

I walked over to a mirrored dresser. Sitting on top were several bottles of expensive perfume. I assumed they were expensive because I had never heard of any of them. I opened a jewelry box and examined its contents. Nothing out of the ordinary. "You buy all this jewelry?" I asked.

"Yes."

"Take a look inside and tell me if there is anything you don't remember buying."

While Herb looked through Bambi's trinkets, I walked around the bed to the picture window that looked out to the beach. I stared through the window at the waves crashing against the sand. "You ever watch *Beachfront Bargain Hunt* on HGTV, Herb?"

"No. Why?"

"Just wondered." I turned and looked down at the floor. There was a large red stain on the beige carpet. It looked an awful lot like blood. Someone had attempted to clean it up. Someone didn't do a very good job. "Who sleeps on this side of the bed?" I asked.

Herb turned toward me. "Bambi sleeps on that side."

"What's this stain on the floor?"

"Oh, that's wine. I knocked an open bottle of wine off the nightstand last night."

I stared into Herb's eyes, thinking, *holy shit this is weird.* "Do you sleep on Bambi's side of the bed when she doesn't come home?"

"Sometimes."

"How often does she not come home?"

"A few times, but never two nights in a row."

"Did you have a fight, Herb?"

"No. Bambi and I rarely argue."

Yeah, really weird. I walked back into the hall and to the locked door. I lifted my foot and kicked it open. The force of the kick sent splinters of wood flying in every direction. The door swung violently open and the doorknob became lodged in the sheetrock.

"What are you doing?" Herb shouted.

"Stay back, Herb." I stepped inside the room. It was empty. No bed, no dressers, and it was the only room without its own bathroom. The walls were painted with only primer and the floor was plywood underlayment. I stood in the middle of the room and slowly turned back toward the door where Herb was standing.

"What exactly are you looking for, Cole?"

"Your dead wife, Herb."

"What do you mean?"

"Herb, this is nuts. Your wife is missing for two days and you don't call the cops. When you speak about her, it's in the past tense, there's a huge stain on your carpet that looks an awful lot like blood, and you're cleaning the entire house like a crime scene cleanup specialist."

"I don't know what to tell you."

"Tell me what you did with your wife's body."

"So you think I killed her?"

"Anyone with half a brain would think you killed her!" I reached into my pocket for my cell phone.

"Cole, what are you doing?"

"I'm going to do what I should have done in the first place. I'm calling the cops."

I started dialing and Herb walked to me and dropped to his knees. "Please, Cole, I'm begging you. Please don't call the cops." He was sobbing and tears were streaming down his face. "I'm begging you, Cole. It's wine!"

"Tommy? It's Cole."

"Hey, Cole. What's up?"

"Tommy, I've got a possible homicide at 4674 Watersong Way."

Chapter Six

After I called the fuzz I brought Herb out front and seated him on the steps. I didn't want him touching anything else or contaminating the crime scene any further … if in fact there was a crime scene at all. He had quit crying but his face and eyes were still red. I heard him whisper, "Why … why," a couple times as he stared at his feet and rocked back and forth.

Tommy Franklin and Dan Kind pulled up first in an unmarked car, and close behind them were two Fort Pierce patrol cars. Before Tommy got out of his car, an ambulance pulled up as well.

Tommy and Kind walked up the driveway. "What do we got, Cole?" Tommy asked.

The two paramedics were pulling a gurney out of the back of the ambulance.

"There's no body, Tommy," I said, nodding my head toward the EMTs.

Tommy put up his hand to halt them. "Hold on with that, guys."

I made introductions. "Tommy, this is Herb Bean. Herb, this is Detective Tommy Franklin and his partner Dan Kind."

Herb looked up and his eyes went from one to the other. He nodded his head in recognition.

"Herb owns the Jetty Lounge, right behind my place," I continued. "His wife hasn't been home in a couple nights."

"Okay," Tommy said. "Has she contacted you in any way?"

Herb shook his head no.

"Can I speak to you inside, Tommy?" I asked.

Tommy looked at Herb. "Do we have your permission to enter the home?"

Herb shook his head yes.

"I need you to say it out loud," Tommy instructed.

"Yes, you have my permission to enter the house … and do whatever you need to do in there."

I turned and walked up the steps. "Thanks, Herb," I said.

"Whatever," Herb replied.

Tommy followed me up the steps and into the house; we went directly up to the bedroom. I explained as much as I could along the way.

"Look at this," I said, pointing at the red stain on the carpet. "Herb says it's wine, and maybe it is."

Tommy glanced down at the stain and then out the front window at the two uniforms in the driveway that were waiting for something to do. "Nice view," he said.

"Ever watch *Beachfront Bargain Hunt*?" I asked.

"Nope. What's with the bedroom door down the hall?"

"That was me. The door was locked and I got a little carried away. For a second there was a part of me that thought his dead wife's body was lying on a bed in that room."

Tommy chuckled. "I'm guessing she wasn't."

"You're correct."

Tommy pulled out his cell phone and placed a call to the Crime Scene Unit. When he hung up he slid the phone back in his pocket. He looked at the photograph of Herb and Bambi on the nightstand. "This our girl?"

I nodded.

"Reminds me of that big-titted blonde from that show," said Tommy.

"That narrows it down," I said.

"The receptionist at that radio station."

"You're thinking about *WKRP in Cincinnati*."

"Yeah. What was her name?"

"Loni Anderson."

"That's her."

"I always liked Bailey better."

"The brunette. Yeah, she was cute. I bet you liked Mary Ann over Ginger too, didn't you?"

"Yup."

Tommy grinned. "Come to think of it, your ex was a Bailey/Mary Ann type."

"Yeah," I grumbled.

"How'd that work out for you?"

"Kiss my ass," I said, and started for the door.

When we got back outside, Tommy told the officers to start a sweep of the immediate area.

"What are we looking for?" one of them asked.

"A clue, dip shit," Tommy replied. He turned to Kind. "Dan, start knocking on some doors, see if anyone has seen anything in the last couple of days that seemed out of place. I'll wait here with Cole till Crime Scene gets here, then I'll join you."

"Roger that," Kind replied, and headed for the nearest neighbor, which was two lots away.

"Can I go back in my house?" Herb called out.

"No," Tommy replied.

"Just hold tight, Herb," I said. "We're waiting for the Crime Scene Unit to arrive."

Herb threw up his arms. "I knew this was going to happen."

Tommy and I just looked at each other.

"How long are they going to take?" Herb asked.

"Hard to say," Tommy answered.

"What if I don't give them permission to enter?"

"Too late," said Tommy. "You allowed me to enter and see that stain on your bedroom carpet."

"It's wine!"

"It's a crime scene."

"What crime?"

"That's what CSU will tell us."

Tommy and I walked toward Herb.

"You guys think I killed her, don't you?" Herb asked.

"Nobody is accusing you of anything, Herb," I replied.

"Not yet any way," said Tommy.

"Should I be looking for a hotel?" Herb asked.

"That's up to you," Tommy said.

"Well, will they be done in there by bedtime?"

"Hard to say."

"Herb, you can stay at my place tonight if need be," I said.

"No thanks, Cole," Herb said, with much sarcasm. "I think you've helped me out enough already."

"Suit yourself."

My cell phone rang and I reached in my pocket to retrieve it. "Hello?"

"Cole, it's Spence."

"Hey, Spence. What's up?"

"You know that guy and his wife you had me run a check on?"

"Yeah."

"They've been married for eight years, and neither have any priors."

"Any history of domestic violence?"

"Not as far as I can tell. No units have ever been dispatched to their current residence or their previous address."

"Where was that?"

"Um … 686 River Terrace in Jensen Beach. It's the home he shared with his first wife."

"*First* wife?"

"Yeah, and that's where things get interesting."

"Interesting, how?"

"Herb Bean was a suspect in the disappearance of his first wife, Jane, back in 2004."

My eyes went to Herb, he was staring over my shoulder at the horizon. "You don't say."

"Yeah, but nobody ever turned up and there was no real evidence against Herb. The case went cold, and he had her declared dead in absentia in 2010, right before he married Bambi."

"Were there any other suspects?"

"None. I also checked into Bambi's background a little. She changed her first *and* last name on the application when she and Herb applied for their marriage license. Her birth name was Veronica Morton. I searched that name and came back with two aliases: Veronica Vegene and Ronnie Lynn."

"Sounds like porn names," I said with a little chuckle.

"That's because they are. She made a few adult films back in '98 and '99 when she was twenty-one and twenty-two."

"What do you mean by 'a few?'"

"Twelve."

"Huh. How did she look in the films, Spence?"

"I ... I, uh ... I didn't watch."

"Aw, come on, Spence." I improvised a few bars of some bow chica wow-wow seventies porn music. "You're a red-blooded American male of *course* you looked."

"I swear, Cole. I didn't watch any of them."

"Yeah, I figured you didn't, Spence. I was just busting your balls."

"Why do you do that to me?"

"Because you're an easy target, Spence," I replied. "And thanks for the foot work, it will help in the investigation."

"Investigation? What investigation?"

"About that. How would you feel about driving out here to Watersong Way real quick?"

"Aw, man."

Chapter Seven

I pulled into Kelly Morgan's driveway around nine on Tuesday morning. On my way from my truck to his front door, I called Leon to tell him I would be late. Just like I knew he would, Leon replied, "Not a problem, boss," and I hung up.

I pounded on the door and turned the knob. The door was unlocked, so I went inside.

"Kelly!" I called out. "Ride's here."

"Hold on!" I heard him shout back from somewhere down the hall.

The television was on and an old episode of *Roseanne* was playing, so I took a seat on the couch and put my feet up on the coffee table and waited.

A few minutes later Kelly limped down the hall; he was still using a cane.

"Ha-ha!" I chuckled. "They really fucked you up, didn't they?"

"Eat a dick," Kelly grumbled.

Kelly's face had healed. The plastic surgeon had done a great job, and the scarring was minimal. He was still using the cane, but his doctors had assured him that with a little more time and therapy, that would be history as well. Considering how badly he was beaten that morning, a few months ago, he was lucky to be alive.

"You ready?" I asked.

"Yeah," he replied. "Just let me grab a cup of coffee to go."

I stood and followed him into the kitchen.

"You want a cup?" he asked.

"Sure," I said.

He reached into one of his base cabinets and pulled out a sleeve of Styrofoam to-go cups and plastic lids. He poured us each a cup and snapped on the lids. I watched his movements; they were slow and deliberate. I even saw him wince a few times. It was obvious he was still in a lot of pain.

"They still have you on any pain medication?" I asked.

He reached above him and pulled open one of the cupboard doors to reveal several prescription bottles. "A whole bunch of shit," he said.

"Is it working?"

"Don't know," he said. "I haven't taken anything in about a week."

"Why?"

"Don't need it."

"Tough guy."

"Just don't think it's a good idea." He shut the cupboard. "I've heard too many stories about people getting addicted to that shit." He handed me my coffee and we walked to the door. I opened the door and turned. Kelly was leaning his cane against the wall.

"Don't you need that?" I asked.

"I'm not going out in public with that goddamn thing."

I nodded my head toward the truck. "After you, tough guy."

He limped to the truck and I followed, keeping an eye on him the whole way. My biggest fear was that he was going to stumble, and I was going to have to help him back to his feet, or worse, have to carry him back to the house. Worse for him, I mean, because I would never let him live that shit down.

My window was down and I paused for a second before turning the key. There was an awful lot of yelling coming from the house next door to Kelly's.

"What's the matter?" Kelly asked.

"You hear that?"

"Hear what?"

"All that yelling coming from next door."

"Oh that. Yeah, I don't even hear it any more. Those two go at it day and night."

"Anyone ever call the cops?"

"Who would call? I don't give shit what goes on over there, and old lady Callahan on the other side is as deaf as a post."

"When did they move in?"

"Six months ago, maybe."

"Should we go over there and see what's going on?"

"No. Why would we do that?"

"To see if she needs help."

Kelly laughed. "She doesn't need any help, trust me."

"What's so funny?"

"He ain't hitting her," Kelly replied. "It's her hitting him. Why do you think the cops are never called? How many guys are gonna call 911 and say, 'Hey can someone come over and help me? My wife is hitting me.'" Kelly chuckled again.

"That's not funny," I said.

"It kinda is."

"No, it's not at all."

"What if that was you?"

"That wouldn't be me. I wouldn't let a woman kick the shit outta me."

"Is he a little guy?" I asked.

"About my size."

"So, that's a yes."

"Screw you."

I started to open my door.

"Don't, Cole," Kelly warned. "I gotta live here."

I stared at the house for a few seconds. The shouting had died down. "Fine," I said. I started the truck and backed out of the driveway.

I took a right onto Sunrise Boulevard. Kelly sipped his coffee and stared out the passenger side window. "Did you hear all three of them took a plea deal?" he asked.

"I heard."

"Bastards. Two days before we were supposed to go to trial."

The *three of them* that Kelly was referring to were Johnny Love—aka Lovey—and his two cronies: Mark Morris, and Clyde Reese Jr. This trio of shitbags broke into Kelly's house and beat the hell out of him. Clyde Reese Jr., or Reese, as his cohorts called him, was the son of the Fellsmere chief of police. It was Chief Reese who gave his son Kelly's address after the younger Reese memorized Kelly's license plate number. Kelly had beat Lovey's ass in a movie theater parking lot a few nights before, when he caught the three young men breaking into his truck.

Reese never gave up his father after he was arrested, and neither did the other two. Kelly and I never mentioned it either, in hopes that someday we would find the opportunity to exact our own form of revenge.

"What did they get?" I asked.

"Sentencing isn't until next week, but Lovey's deal was for five years, and the other two would receive three years."

"How does that sit with you?"

"I wish they were all given the death penalty," Kelly replied. "But what are you going to do?"

"Yeah, what are you going to do," I repeated.

"Hanging them in the village square would have been nice."

"I'm pretty sure they don't do that in Florida anymore."

"Probably not," Kelly sighed. "I don't even know if Fort Pierce has a village square."

Kelly was silent for the rest of the ride, but when we pulled into Dr. Stevens' parking lot, he turned to me and asked, "Do we still plan on paying a visit to Chief Clyde Reese?"

I reached over and put my hand on his shoulder. "When you're fully recovered, we'll take a ride over to Fellsmeer."

"Thanks," Kelly said with a nod. "Now get your hand off me. I've told you before, I'm not gonna have sex with you."

I squeezed his shoulder. "Don't flatter yourself, you ugly bastard. I think I could do a lot better than you."

Chapter Eight

After Kelly's appointment I convinced him to swing by the Breakwater with me for a bite to eat. He tried his hardest to argue, but he wasn't driving, so of course I won that argument. It was his first time at the Breakwater since his attack, and I thought it might do him some good to get out around other people.

When we drove past the Jetty Lounge, Herb was standing in the parking lot next to his Lincoln reading a paper. He glanced up when he heard the truck going by. I waved. Herb didn't wave back; he just looked back down at the paper. He was probably still mad at me for calling Tommy Franklin, but what other choice did I have?

"What's Herbs problem?" Kelly asked, noticing the little guy hadn't returned my wave.

"That, my friend, is a story I'm going to tell you at the picnic table over a couple beers," I replied.

"I can hardly wait."

I whipped into the only empty spot in front of the Breakwater, and we got out of the truck. Kelly gave me a look over the hood.

"What's the matter?" I asked.

"I don't know," Kelly replied. "I just haven't been in here in a while."

"You'll be fine."

As we neared the door, he paused again. "Am I limping badly?" he asked.

"Hardly noticeable," I lied.

"Yeah right." Kelly pulled open the door, took a deep breath, and went inside.

"Holy shit! Melvin hollered. "Look what the cat dragged in."

"Yeah, yeah," Kelly said. He winced as he boarded his stool.

"Long time, no see." Melvin reached across the two stools that separated them. "Did you get shorter since the last time I saw you?"

Kelly shook Melvin's hand. "It's good to be back, Melvin," he said. "And fuck you."

Melvin laughed out loud. His face turned blue, his shoulders shook, and the whites of his eyes turned red. We all paused and waited to see if this was the laugh that would finally do the old bastard in. It wasn't. He finally took a deep breath and his gray coloring returned to his face.

"All kidding aside," Melvin said, "it's good to have you back. How ya feelin' ... besides that horrible limp I mean?"

"I feel a little better every day," said Kelly.

"You think they would have given you a cane to help you walk."

"I don't need no cane," Kelly shot back.

I placed two Bud Lights on the bar. "Bullshit," I said. "They gave him a cane. He only uses it at home. Says he's too embarrassed to go out in public with it."

Kelly shot me a look. "Thanks asshole."

"You're welcome." I pushed Kelly's beer across the bar to him. He grabbed it by the neck and up ended it.

"*Ahh*, that's good," Kelly said.

"Sounds like it's been awhile," said Melvin.

"Yeah, I wasn't supposed to drink booze with any of the medication I was on."

"Bah," Melvin responded, waving an argumentative hand at him. "A little pills and booze never hurt no one."

Kelly cocked his head as he stared at the old man. "Actually, Melvin—never mind."

Melvin downed the rest of his drink and pushed the glass to the edge of the bar. "I'll tell you what," he said. "I'll let you buy me one drink as a welcome back gift."

"Thanks," Kelly said. "You're all heart."

The door opened and in walked Franklin and Kind.

"What's up, Tommy?" I said.

The two detectives took the two seats between Melvin and Kelly. Tommy Franklin pointed at Kelly. "Morgan, right?" he asked.

"Yeah," Kelly replied.

"You're the one who got his ass kicked."

"That's me."

"How you doing with that?"

"I'm gettin' there."

"I see Lovey and the boys pled out."

Kelly nodded.

"Can I get you gentlemen something to drink?" I asked.

"I'll take a coffee, Cole," Tommy said.

"Same here," said Kind.

I looked around for someone I could pass the order too, but no one was around. "I'll be right back with those," I said.

I returned a couple minutes later with their cups and placed them on the bar. "So what brings you guys in for a second day in a row?" I asked.

"We were headed next door to your buddy's place to ask him a few more questions," Tommy answered, "but I needed a cup of coffee first."

"Herb's not my buddy," I said. "He's just a guy I share a dumpster with."

Tommy grinned. "I think ol' Herb's been sharing more than his dumpster."

"If ya know what he means," added Kind.

"Yeah ... I know what he means," I assured him.

"I'm talking about his wife," said Kind.

"Yeah, I know," I said.

Tommy sipped his coffee. "Your son-in-law was a little pissed at me. Said I stole the case from him."

"You kinda did," I said.

"It's first one on the scene, not first one who talks about it," Tommy argued.

I shrugged. "He'll get over it. Dig up anything else?"

"Yes. Our missing lady was arrested back in '92."

I thought for a second. "She would have been fifteen."

"Which is why her record was sealed. We're trying to get a judge to release her file."

"But no one will release it because she isn't the one who is suspected of committing a crime," I surmised.

"Correct. So we're going over to ask Herb if he knows why she was arrested, or if he even knows she was." Tommy gulped down the rest of his coffee and backed off his stool. "Well, we better get going."

"When you questioned him the first time," I asked, "did he know about the films she had appeared in?"

"Yes," Kind answered. "Only he referred to them as art films."

"So then she's not a porn star," I said. "She's an artist."

Tommy nodded his head. "I have to agree, Cole. I watched one of her movies last night—you know, for the case—and the woman *is* an artist."

"Yeah, for the case," I said sarcastically.

Tommy and Kind headed for the door. Tommy turned as he got there. "Tell Spence thanks for all his help on this one."

"He'll appreciate hearing that."

"Yeah, I bet he will."

Chapter Nine

It was Thursday morning around nine thirty when I returned to my favorite Circle K. I could have paid at the pump with my debit card, but once again, I went inside to pay. I figured lightening never strikes twice.

There was a woman in line ahead of me buying scratch-offs, and while I waited in line I looked around the store. There was a faint bloodstain where the biker had been shot, and another very small one where the old man's blood had seeped under the checkout counter. No one else would have known what they were or maybe even noticed them for that matter.

The woman ahead of me turned and left and I stepped up to the counter. "Thirty dollars on pump two," I said.

The young kid behind the counter with a name tag that read Jim glanced out the window. "The F-150?" he asked.

"That's the one," I replied. I tossed a twenty and a ten onto the counter, turned and walked out the door.

When I was halfway across the parking lot, I noticed a young girl standing to my right, in the grass median, near a palmetto tree, between the parking lot and Thirty-Fifth Street. The teen was dressed in black denim shorts, a white tank top, and cowboy boots. She had a long-sleeved flannel shirt tied around her waist and a small backpack thrown over one shoulder. She stood motionless staring at the building with her arms at her sides. I kept my eye on her and wondered what she was doing as I crossed the parking lot toward my truck. There was something familiar about the young brunette, but I couldn't put my finger on it. Where had I seen this girl before? She noticed me and gave me one of those *what-are-you-looking-at-ya-perv* glares.

I pulled open the truck door, and climbed in. I drove out onto Virginia Avenue and took a right. As I crossed through the intersection I glanced back over at the girl; she was still standing there.

I made it a few blocks when it dawned on me why she looked so familiar. She had to be Josh Sanders' sister; the resemblance was remarkable. *What was that name Tommy gave me? Lacey, that was it.* I took a right onto Thirtieth Street, and then another at Cortez Boulevard. It took me a few minutes to get back to the Circle K; I had to drive all the way around Indian River College. When I arrived back at the gas station, the girl had already crossed Virginia Avenue and was heading north down Thirty-Fifth. She walked in the road against traffic. She walked with her shoulders back and her arms out like she was a tough little ass kicker. I waited for the light to change and went through the intersection. I drove about twenty yards past her and pulled to the side of the road. I got out of the truck and started across the street. The young girl paused. She puffed out her chest. I wondered if she really thought she could intimidate me.

I put up my hands. "Lacey?" I asked.

"Don't come any closer, asshole," she ordered.

I kept moving toward her. "Are you Lacey Sanders?" I asked.

"Fuck off!"

"I'll take that as a maybe. I knew your grandfather and brother," I said, taking a step.

"I told you not to come any closer."

I wished I had listened, because right when I got close enough, I received a quick-as-lightning cowboy boot to the nuts. I dropped to my knees in the dirt, grabbed my balls and groaned. That's when I took a right to the cheek. It was a damn good right. That kid could swing a fist.

"Son of a bitch!" I wheezed.

Lacey took off running.

"Wait!" I hollered.

She didn't wait. By the time I staggered to my feet and turned around, she was headed down Sarasota Avenue.

I limped back to my truck. I could have let her go, but the cop in me wasn't about to let that little turd get the best of me. I spun the tires and started back up Thirty-Fifth Avenue. When I took the right onto Sarasota, I saw Lacey run into a small wooded area behind some houses, across from the elementary school. I pulled to the curb and got out. My nuts had descended from my throat back down to where they belonged as I gave chase, still limping a little.

I caught up with Lacey just as we exited the woods. There was a culvert ditch between us and Virginia Avenue. Lacey paused and I dove for the flannel shirt that was around her waist, yanking her to the dirt.

Lacey swung her fists wildly and kicked at me. "Get off me, you pervert!" she screamed. "Help! Help!"

I straddled her legs and pinned her arms to the ground, mainly for my own protection. "Knock it off!" I yelled in my best cop voice. Lacey froze. "Listen, I'm not going to hurt you. I just wanted to talk."

"That's even more creepy," she said.

"I'm a cop," I said. "I'm going to let you up, but don't run. Okay?"

She nodded yes.

I got up, and as I did I protected the old family jewels in case there was another kick coming my way. Lacey climbed to her feet as well.

"What do you want with me?"

"You are Lacey Sanders, aren't you?"

"Who wants to know?"

I looked around. "Well, I'm the only one here, so, I want to know."

Just then two guys in their thirties exited the woods about twenty feet east of us. One guy was wearing jeans with no shirt, and he was barefoot. The other guy wore a black T-shirt, jeans, and work boots. They must have come from one of the houses at the edge of the woods.

"You okay?" Work Boots hollered.

"Everything is fine," I shouted back. They kept walking toward us.

"We weren't askin' you," the other one said. "We was askin' the young lady."

"She's fine," I said.

Lacey gave me a quick grin, turned and ran toward the two men. "He tried to rape me," she sobbed.

I rolled my eyes. "I didn't try to rape her. I'm a cop."

"Let's see some ID," said No Shirt.

I reached for my wallet. It was gone. *Shit!* I looked around the ground near me. "I must have lost it."

Work Boots smiled. "Sure ya did."

Lacey had her face buried in Work Boot's chest. Her shoulders shook as she pretended to cry. He patted her on the back.

No Shirt bent down and picked up a broken tree branch. The branch was about as big around as the grip end of a baseball bat. He moved slowly toward me and to my left.

Work Boots grabbed Lacey by the shoulder and moved her to the side. "You let us take care of this guy, sweetheart," he said. Then he started toward me as well; he moved to my right.

Lacey turned around and stared at me; the little shit was grinning big. She folded her arms across her chest and waited for the show she was directing.

No Shirt swung first. I put up my arm to block the branch; it snapped in half. Luckily the branch was long dead, or it would have been my forearm that snapped.

I gave No Shirt a hard right to the cheek. It dazed him and he took two steps back. The look in his eye told me he wasn't expecting to be hit that hard.

Work Boots moved in. I stepped back and gave him an elbow to the nose. I heard the crack and the blood exploded from his nostrils. He grabbed his nose and cried out.

I turned back to No Shirt; he was coming in for more. I brought up the palm of my right hand as hard as I could, catching him under the chin. His head snapped violently back, and he swayed for a long moment before toppling backwards into the bed of pine needles.

With No Shirt out cold, I returned my attention to Work Boots.

Work boots held his nose with one hand and put up the other hand in surrender.

"Seriously?" I asked. "That's all you got? You're almost twenty years younger than me. You should be ashamed of yourself." I glared at Lacey and pointed back the way we had come. "Let's go."

She dropped her arms back to her sides and relaxed her shoulders. "Fine," she said.

The two of us walked quietly back to my truck. I found my wallet lying in the grass on the way. I opened the door for Lacey, and she got in. I got in and started the truck.

"Was that fun?" I asked angrily.

"Was what fun?"

"Making me kick the shit out of those two guys."

"It was kinda funny."

"No, it wasn't." I put the truck in drive and we headed down the street.

Chapter Ten

I called Tommy Franklin from my truck and had him meet us at the Fort Pierce Police Department. Lacey wasn't very happy about that because, in her words, "I hate all pigs." I didn't take it personally, because I was just a retired pig.

Tommy's interview with Lacey produced some interesting revelations. Tommy questioned Lacey about her brother and grandfather, both of whom, we found out, she hadn't seen in over a year. She only came back to Fort Pierce when she saw a story about the holdup on the local news in Ocala, where she was living at the time. She didn't even know her mother had passed away until we told her. The news really took the wind out of her sails. For the first time since I had met Lacey, she didn't look so tough.

Tommy walked the two of us out to the parking lot when we were finished.

"What are you going to do with her?" Tommy asked.

I watched her cross the parking lot and climb back into my truck. "I have no idea."

"I can call child protective services if you want me to."

"She's going to be eighteen in a month."

Tommy slapped me on the back. "You get into more shit since you retired."

"No kidding," I responded.

I pulled out of the parking lot and took a right onto Third Street. "You hungry?" I asked.

She shrugged her shoulders.

"When did you eat last?" I asked.

"Last night," Lacey said.

I brought her to the Breakwater. There were no parking spots out front, so I drove around Jetty Park and found a spot on the other side of the park. I backed in and shut off the engine.

"What are we doing here?" Lacey asked.

"Getting you something to eat," I replied.

"I only got thirty bucks," she informed me.

"That should get you some lunch."

We got out and walked across the park. As we neared the Breakwater, a slight smirk appeared on Lacey's face.

"What's so funny?" I asked.

"It's nothing."

"It's something."

"Me and my friends used to steal beer from this place."

"The Breakwater?" I asked, pointing ahead.

"Yeah. There's an outside entrance to the walk-in cooler. We would break in after they closed and take a case or two. We never took too much, so the moron who owned the place never caught on."

"How long ago was that?"

"Three years, I guess." Lacey walked to the alley and poked her head around the corner. "Huh. The door used to be right there."

"Yeah," I said. "It was. I had it removed a couple years ago because I thought someone was stealing beer."

Lacey's head snapped around. "You removed it?"

"I own the place. I was the moron."

"Shit."

"Yeah, shit."

"Sorry."

"Are you?"

Lacey gave me another one of her shrugs that was quickly becoming her trademark. "Not really, I guess." She turned and went to the front door. I pulled it open and she went inside.

Allison was behind the bar, Melvin was on his favorite stool sipping a Scotch with a lemon twist, and Spence sat a few stools down from him eating a BLT.

"Who's on?" I asked.

"Norma and Emily," Allison replied, as she looked Lacey up and down.

"Take a picture, it'll last longer," Lacey said to Allison.

Allison looked to me for answers.

"This is Lacey Sanders," I announced. "It was her brother who tried to rob the Circle K Monday morning." Everyone was now more confused than when we walked through the door. "It was her grandfather who was working the register and was shot and killed," I added.

No one said anything. Their eyes followed Lacey as she crossed the floor and perched on one of the barstools between Melvin and Spence.

"Bud Light," Lacey ordered.

Allison's eyes went back to me.

"And she's only seventeen," I said.

Lacey gave me a dirty look. "Fine. Just give me a Coke."

Allison poured the drink and set it on the bar in front of Lacey. "I'm very sorry for your loss," she said.

"Why?" Allison asked. "You didn't kill him."

"Lacey," I said, "this is my daughter Allison. That's Melvin at the end of the bar, and this is Spence."

"My boyfriend," Allison said territorially.

Lacey nodded to each one as I named them. "So, what do you got to eat in this dump?" she asked.

Allison laid a menu on the bar next to her soda. Lacey picked up the menu and skimmed over the three pages. "I'll have a cheeseburger and fries," she said.

Allison wrote it on a ticket. "Coming right up," she said with the fakest of smiles, and walked to the kitchen. Lacey returned the same smile.

When Allison came back to the bar I told her to keep an eye on things while I walked over to the Jetty Lounge.

I hadn't noticed when Lacey and I drove by, but the Jetty Lounge was dark, and there was a closed sign in the window. When I got closer to the door, I noticed there was also a note taped to the glass. CLOSED UNTIL FURTHER NOTICE, the note read. I looked around; Herb's car wasn't in the parking lot.

I took out my cell phone and dialed Herb's number; I got his voicemail. "Herb, it's Cole. Hey, I'm at your restaurant. I haven't heard from you in a couple days and I was just wondering how you were doing. Uh … give me a call back when you get this." I hung up the cell and dropped it back in my pocket. I thought about calling Tommy, but I had just seen him at the station earlier, and he said then that there was nothing new on Bambi's disappearance. I walked back to the Breakwater. The whole way back I thought about Herb, and how Tommy had told me that the stain on the carpet really was red wine. Herb looked pretty damn guilty—the husband usually does—but there was no real evidence pointing to foul play of any kind. The $64,000 questioned remained: where was Bambi Bean? It had been five days now since she was last seen, and as every cop knows, the chances of solving a case like this drops substantially after the first forty-eight hours.

Tommy also told me that video surveillance obtained from the five Publix super markets nearest to the Beans' home showed no sign of Bambi entering or exiting any of those locations. She had either lied to Herb about where she was going, chosen another grocery store, or was abducted before reaching the Publix. Traffic cameras and video surveillance from other grocery stores were being gathered, but it would take days to go through all the footage. I could only imagine what Herb was going through.

When I returned to the Breakwater, Lacey was gone. My eyes went from her empty stool to Allison. "Where did she go?" I asked.

"She left," Allison replied.

"Did she eat?"

"She took it with her."

I walked back toward the door.

Allison pointed at the door that led out to the beach. "She went that-a-way."

I changed directions and walked out the side door. I went out past the volleyball nets and picnic tables to the hill that overlooked the beach. I looked up the beach in one direction and down the beach in the other. She was nowhere in sight. I stood there for another five minutes or so, my eyes focusing on one young girl after another. Where did she go? Why did I even care? I looked down at the sand beneath my feet and wondered where my own daughter Angel was. It had been three days since I heard from her. I wondered if she had eaten. I wondered if she was even alive.

"Hey."

I turned my head to see Tommy Franklin walking toward me; he was alone. "What's up?" I said.

"You see your buddy lately?"

"Kelly Morgan?" I asked.

"Herb Bean," he replied.

"He ain't my buddy. And no, I haven't seen him. Why?"

"Because I phoned him yesterday afternoon. I got his voicemail and told him to call me when he got the message. He never called back, so I took a ride out to his place after you and that Sanders girl left the station. He wasn't there, and I see he has closed down the restaurant."

"Weird," I said. "Herb sure doesn't seem like a flight risk."

"He also doesn't seem like a guy who would misplace a wife every few years."

"No, he doesn't," I agreed. I looked back in the direction of the Breakwater. "Where's your partner?"

"He's sitting at the bar."

"Flirting with my daughter?"

"Probably."

"Maybe we better head back inside before he does something stupid and I have to shoot him."

"Good idea."

We both turned and started walking back. As we walked along, Tommy asked, "What happened to that Sanders kid?"

"I brought her back here, fed her, and then she snuck out when I wasn't looking."

"She pay the check?"

"No."

"Kids."

"Yeah, kids."

Chapter Eleven

Frank and Poco, two bikers who usually stopped in on Thursdays and Sundays, were the last two in the bar. They were drinking LandShark Lagers. Frank had eaten a cheeseburger earlier in the night, but Poco said he was meeting his girlfriend around eight and they were grabbing something to eat together. Eight came and went, and Poco never left, so I don't know what that was all about.

The kitchen lights shut off and out walked Leon. "Takin' off, boss," he said.

"See you in the morning, Leon," I said.

As Leon walked past Frank and Poco he said, "What up, gentlemen?" He put up his hand and both bikers gave him the proverbial high five.

"Hey, Leon," they both replied together.

"How's it going?" Frank asked.

"Oh, you know, same day, different pile of dog shit," Leon shot back. He went out the door and strutted across

Jetty Park to his car like a graduate from the George Jefferson School of Walking Perfection.

Frank downed his beer and slid off the back of his stool. "Come on, man," he said. "Down that beer. We gotta get going."

"Yeah, yeah," said Poco. He gulped down the last of his Landshark and looked back over his shoulder at the clock. "Holy shit. Is that the real time?"

"It is," I replied with a nod.

"Damn," Poco said. "Maggie is gonna be *pi*-issed."

Frank slapped him on the back. "Ain't the first time, amigo."

"And it sure as hell won't be the last," said Poco.

They both said their good byes, and out the door they went.

I pulled the chains on the neon beer signs that hung in the window and then went to the kitchen to make sure everything had been shut off. I checked the stove, the pizza oven, and the range hood. Like every other night, Leon hadn't forgotten anything. I gave the back door a good jiggle to make sure it was locked, and then did the same thing with the door to the walk-in cooler.

When I returned to the bar, Lacey Sanders was sitting on one of the bar stools sipping a bottle of Bud Light.

"Stealing my beer again?" I asked.

"No," she said, and slid a twenty-dollar bill down the bar. "Take my burger and fries outta that too."

"The grub was on me, and I can't sell you the beer because you're a minor."

Lacey took another sip. "You didn't tell me you were the one who put my brother in the hospital."

"I was going to tell you, but I was waiting for the right time."

"When's the right time to tell someone you busted their brother's skull with a soup can?"

"I don't know. I've only taken people down with a gun, and a few times with a night stick."

"He's still unconscious."

"I know."

"How do you know?"

"I called the hospital this afternoon."

"Because you were worried about him?"

"No. I don't give a shit about him, but I was worried about you."

Lacey laughed. "Worried about me, huh?"

I walked around the bar and grabbed a beer for myself. "Did you go to the hospital and see him?" I asked. I popped the top, leaned against the back bar, and took a big gulp.

"Yes. The doctor says he has traumatic brain injury, and he might not be the same when he wakes up."

"That's what they told me too."

Lacey shrugged. "No one would be able to tell if he had a brain injury; he was always a goddamn moron anyway."

I tried not to laugh, but that was kinda funny.

"He's going to spend the rest of his life in prison, isn't he?" Lacey asked.

"Yes."

"You should have just killed him."

"If I had my weapon on me, I would have."

"Do you think my grandfather was in on it?"

"Yes."

"Do you think Josh shot him on purpose?"

"No."

"I don't think so either."

"Where are you staying tonight?" I asked.

"I don't know."

"Do you have any more money?"

"Fourteen or fifteen dollars, maybe."

"Do you have any friends you can stay with?"

"Not really."

"You can stay at my place tonight if you would like."

Lacey looked up from her bottle. "Why are you being so nice to me?"

"Because I have daughters, and if I wasn't around, I would hope somebody would be nice to them."

"I bet you don't have a daughter who's as fucked up as me."

"I have a daughter who's much more fucked up than you … and I hope someone is being nice to her right now."

"Do you live in a house or an apartment?"

"Does it matter?"

"No, just wondering. Can I have another beer?"

"No."

"Why?"

"Because you're only seventeen."

"So? I started drinking when I was fourteen."

"So did I."

"Then what's the big deal?"

"It's against the law."

"You said you weren't a cop anymore."

"No. I said I was a retired cop."

"And once a cop, always a cop."

I smiled. "That's right, now drink down the rest of that beer so I can lock up."

Lacey hopped off the bar stool and we walked outside. I locked the door behind us and started in the direction of my truck. "If you want to stay at my place," I said, "then come on. If not, there's a bench right over there in the park."

Lacey ran to catch up with me. "You're kind of a jerk," she said.

"Yup," I replied.

"I like that about you."

Chapter Twelve

My cell phone started ringing around five o'clock on Friday morning. When you're a father you hate phone calls at odd hours, especially if you have a daughter like my Angel. I shot up in bed and grabbed the cell quicker than my eyes could focus. I stared at the caller ID, blinking and squinting trying to read the numbers. When my vision cleared, I saw that it was Howard Bean.

"Herb, why the hell are you calling me at this hour?"

"I need your help."

"Again? What did you do, run out and get a new wife, and now she's missing too?"

"Seriously, Cole, I need your help with something."

"I don't help bury bodies, Herb."

"I got a phone call late last night."

"Detective Franklin has been trying to get a hold of you."

"I know. I haven't been returning his phone calls."

"Why not?"

"Because it's just like I said it would be, they're concentrating on me instead of finding out what happened to Bambi. I'm their number one suspect. I'm through with the police."

"Well, they might not be through with you, Herb."

"Are you going to listen to me, or not?"

"I guess, but hurry it up. I would like to get back to sleep."

"I got a call late last night … from a guy."

"What guy?"

"I don't know who he was."

"What did he say?"

"He said he has Bambi."

"Has her?"

"He kidnapped her."

I rolled my eyes. I don't know why. Herb wasn't there to see it. "Why would this guy wait almost a week to contact you?"

"How would I know?"

"Herb, call Detective Franklin."

"Herb sighed loudly.

Huh, I thought. *I should have gone with the sigh instead of the eye roll*.

"I'm not calling the police, Cole. He said that if I did, he would kill her. If you won't help me, I'll do what I have to do on my own."

"They always tell you not to call the police, Herb, but the chances of recovering an abduction victim are dramatically higher when the police are involved."

"He called me from Bambi's phone, Cole."

"So you think that Franklin will think you made the call yourself."

"Yes."

"Because you've seen it before on *Forensic Files*."

"Yes."

"They can tell where the call originated from, Herb."

"And I would have been smart enough to drive somewhere before making the call."

"Yeah. That reminds me, where have you been the last couple of days?"

Herb sighed again, but this time it was more of a moan. "Here we go again," he said.

I pulled back the covers and got out of bed. "Are you home, Herb?"

"Yes."

"I'll be right there."

"Thanks, Cole."

"Don't thank me yet." I hung up the cell and tossed it on the bed. I picked up my cargo shorts from the day before and put them on. I grabbed a T-shirt that was hanging in the closet and put that on as well. I grabbed my cell, dropped it into my pocket, and headed down the hallway.

I knocked lightly on the guest room door, and listened for stirring; there was nothing. I knocked again, this time a little louder.

"Yeah?" Lacey called out.

"Can I open the door?" I asked.

"Why?"

I opened the door a crack and peeked inside the room. "Hey, I got a call. I have to leave for a little while."

"Is it your daughter?"

"No, just some idiot."

I heard her giggle. "Okay."

"I should be back in a couple hours. If I'm not, there's breakfast cereal in the cupboard and eggs in the fridge. Help yourself."

"Okay. Thank you, Cole."

"Yup." I pulled the door closed and started the search for my truck keys.

Chapter Thirteen

It was almost six when I got to Herb's place. I pulled into the driveway and got out. The sun wouldn't be coming up for another forty-five minutes or so. There was only one light on in Herb's house.

My .38 revolver was small enough to fit in one of the large pockets of my cargo shorts. As I walked up Herb's steps I reached into the pocket and adjusted the weapon, and then tucked the flap inside the pocket. I hoped I wouldn't need it, but it was there if I did.

I wrapped on the door and then hit the doorbell button. I could hear Herb's bare feet slap the tiled floor as he ran to answer the door. The knob turned and he yanked it open.

"Cole! Thank God," he said.

"Yeah, thank God," I responded.

Herb pulled the door all the way open. He backed up and motioned me in.

"What time did *the guy* call?" I asked. I made finger quotes when I said 'the guy.' I don't know if I did it because Herb had referred to the caller as 'the guy,' or because I thought the guy was probably imaginary.

"He called last night, around eleven," Herb replied.

"Around eleven?"

Herb put up his index finger. "Wait a minute." He ran to the kitchen for his cell phone and checked the call log. "It was exactly eleven twenty-two, and we spoke for four minutes."

I followed him into the kitchen. "The police will be able to tell if both phones were in the same location during the call."

"I know, but I would have been smart enough to pay someone to be here to answer my phone."

"You've got all the answers, Herb."

"*Forensic Fi—*"

"I know. *Forensic Files*. What exactly did this man say?"

"He said he has Bambi, and that he'll call me this evening at five with instructions. He said if I call the police he'll kill her."

"Did he say what he wants?"

"No." Herb turned and walked to the kitchen table. He pulled out the chair at the end of the table and sat down. He put his elbows on the table and rested his forehead in the palms of his hands.

"He didn't ask for a ransom?"

"No. When I asked him what he wanted, he said he would let me know."

"This all sounds a little fishy, Herb."

"Fishy, how?"

"No one abducts a person and then waits almost a week to contact their family, and when they do call, they ask for something … usually money."

"I don't know what to tell you, Cole."

"Think, Herb, did he say anything else?"

"No!" Herb continued to stare at the table top. "Wait. Yes, he did say something else."

"What did he say, Herb?"

"He said something about payback."

"Okay. What did he say?"

"He said, 'Payback's a bitch.'"

I cocked my head. "Really, Herb? He said payback's a bitch?"

"Yeah, why?"

"It just sounds a little cliché, Herb."

"What do you mean?"

"People don't really say payback's a bitch all that often in real life. It's more like something people would say in a movie. I doubt Clint Eastwood or Sylvester Stallone kidnapped your wife."

"I don't know wha—"

"I know, Herb, you don't know what to tell me."

I pulled out my cell phone and snapped a picture of Herb.

"Why did you take a picture of me?"

"Just so I would have it. Do you have a photograph of Bambi on your cell?"

"Yes. I'm sure I do."

"Text it to me."

"What are you going to do now?"

"I'm going home to eat some breakfast. I'll be back here around four-thirty."

"What do you want me to do?"

"I don't care." I walked back down the hall to the front door; Herb followed.

As I walked down the steps, Herb stood at the open door. "Thanks, Cole," he said.

"Yeah," I replied, with a wave of my hand.

I backed out of Herb's driveway and headed home. As I drove along, "payback's a bitch" kept running through my mind. I decided to give Tommy Franklin a call.

"Hello?" Tommy answered.

"Hey, it's Cole," I said.

"I was just going to call you."

"Oh yeah?"

"Yeah. You hear from Herb Bean yet?"

"Nope," I lied. "Why do you ask?"

"We got a hit off his wife's cell phone late last night."

"You know where the call originated from?"

"A bar on Indian River Drive in Sebastian called Earl's Hideaway. I notified the Sebastian Police Department. They're pulling video surveillance from a Publix that's four miles down the road from the bar. I have to run up there and pick it up around noon. If you hear from Bean let me know."

"I sure will."

"I'm going to head over to his place now and see if he's there."

We hung up and I called Herb to let him know that Tommy would be paying him a visit. I know I shouldn't have, but I think I was starting to believe Herb's story. Herb thanked me once again and we hung up. A few seconds later I got a text from him; it was a photograph of Bambi. Why he sent me a photograph of his wife in a skimpy white bikini I'll never know. Maybe it was the only picture he had on his cell. *Wow*, I thought. W*hat a body*. I stared at the pic for a second and almost ran head on into a tractor trailer. I swerved back into my lane at the last second. Maybe Herb sent me that particular photograph to try to kill me.

Chapter Fourteen

When I arrived back at my apartment, Lacey had already showered and gotten dressed. I asked her if she would like me to make her a couple eggs and some bacon. She declined the offer and said cereal would be fine. We sat together at my kitchen table and each had a bowl of Cap'n Crunch Peanut Butter Crunch. She remarked that she hadn't had it since she was a kid. I told her it was one of my favorites. For some reason that surprised her. She said she thought old people only ate Cheerios and Shredded Wheat. I told her I wasn't that old. She laughed and assured me I was.

We finished breakfast, and I put both bowls in the sink and rinsed out the residue. "I have to go to the restaurant this morning, and then I have to be somewhere at four thirty," I commented. "Do you want to stick around here, or would you like me to drop you off somewhere?"

"Can you drop me off at the hospital? I want to see my brother one more time before I head back up to Ocala."

"Sure, I can do that."

"Then I'll just walk over to the bus station from there."

"The bus station is four or five miles from the hospital."

"So. I've walked farther than five miles before."

"How about if I wait at the hospital, and then I'll take you to the bus station?"

"If you want to."

"I do."

Lacey grabbed her backpack and we drove to the hospital. I waited outside her brother's room with the police officer that was stationed at the door. Josh still hadn't regained consciousness. I could hear Lacey speaking to him from the hall. She told him she loved him, and that she would try to come see him wherever he ended up. She walked back into the hall.

"You good?" I asked.

"Yup," she said.

"Shall we hit the road?"

"Yup."

Fifteen minutes later I pulled off of Okeechobee Road and parked in the parking lot of the Greyhound Bus Terminal. I walked Lacey inside. I purchased her a one-way ticket to Ocala and gave her an extra fifty-dollar bill.

"Here," I said, handing her the fifty. "Grab some lunch later, or something."

She put her arms around me and gave me a big hug. "Thanks for everything," she said.

"No problem," I replied. I handed her a business card. "If you ever need anything, just give me a call."

"You're a real nice guy … for a pig who's kind of a jerk." She smiled, turned, and walked away.

I was almost to my truck when my cell phone rang. "Yeah, Herb?" I answered.

"He called back," Herb said.

"It's only nine o'clock."

"I know."

"What did he say?"

"He said he wants $100,000."

"Where are you?"

"At Jetty Park. Where are you?"

"I'm on my way, Herb. Stay right there."

Chapter Fifteen

I spotted Herb's car on the far side of Jetty Park, directly across from the Breakwater. I drove around the park and pulled into a spot right next to him. He was already out of his car when I got there.

"What time did he call, Herb?" I asked.

"Right before I called you," Herb replied. "As soon as he hung up, I dialed your number."

I held out my hand. "Give me your phone, Herb."

He looked confused. "Okay," he said, and handed it to me.

I pulled up his call log. There was a call four minutes before his call to me. The call was labeled Bambi. "He's still using Bambi's phone?"

"Yes."

"And he asked for a hundred grand?"

"Yes."

"Do you have a hundred grand, Herb?"

"Yes. It's in a paper bag in my trunk."

"You just had a hundred grand lying around?"

"Well, it was in my safe, it wasn't just lying around."

"When and where does he want it?"

Herb pulled a folded piece of yellow legal paper out of the back pocket of his Dockers and handed it to me. "Here, I wrote it down."

I unfolded the paper. In pencil, Herb had written,

Put money in Bambi's car. Noon.

Right off Sebastian Blvd onto WW Ranch Rd.

Follow 3 and a half miles to pond.

DO NOT take 95.

I looked up at Herb. His face was pale, and sweat beads were forming along his departed hairline. "You know where this place is?" I asked.

"I know where Sebastian Road is," he replied.

"What does this mean, *Put money in Bambi's car*?"

"He said Bambi's car will be in the parking lot of the Melbourne Square Mall. It will be parked in front of Dick's Sporting Goods. We're supposed to put the money in a bag and put in the backseat and lock the door. Then go to the end of WW Ranch Road. Bambi will be waiting there for me."

"Did he say why we can't take I-95?"

"No, but he said someone would be watching, and if we do, she's dead."

I took a deep breath and exhaled. "Herb, we don't even know if she *is* alive. We should call back and ask for proof of life."

"I asked to speak to her, but he wouldn't let me. Also, he told me he was going to smash her cell the second he got off the phone with me."

I pulled up Google Maps on my cell phone. It would take us an hour and twenty minutes to get to Melbourne Square Mall, and then another forty-five minutes to get to the pond at the end of Ranch Road. "We should call Detective Franklin," I said.

"They said, 'No cops.'"

"They? What do you mean, *they*?"

"Well there must be more than one of them. Someone has to be watching the parking lot, and someone will be making sure we don't take I-95."

"If Bambi is already at the site then one guy could do it all."

"I guess," Herb responded.

"Herb, is there anything you're not telling me?"

"No, Cole, I swear on Bambi's life."

I thought that was a weird thing for Heb to say, because either he truly believed she was still alive, or he knew she wasn't, and swearing on her life meant nothing to him. *Which is it Herb*, I thought.

"What time is it?" I asked.

Herb looked at his wristwatch. "Almost ten," he said.

I grabbed my cell again and dialed Kelly Morgan's number.

"Hello?" Kelly said.

"Hey, it's Cole."

"What's up?"

"How are you feeling?"

"Fine. Why?"

"Your neurologist clear you to drive yet?"

"My appointment isn't until Monday. Why?"

"You feel like driving anyway?"

"What the hell is this all about, Cole?"

"Yes or no?"

"I guess," Kelly replied with a sigh. "Where do you want me?"

"Be to the Breakwater in twenty minutes."

"Twenty minutes? I'm still in my pajamas."

"Twenty minutes," I repeated, and hung up. I started walking down one of the sidewalks that wound through Jetty Park. "Come on."

"Where we going?" Herb asked, as he hurried to catch up.

"I have to grab something out of my office."

"What?"

"My .357."

Chapter Sixteen

Herb and I headed up US1 toward Melbourne in my F-150, with Kelly following in his. I told him to stay far enough back that no one could tell we were being followed. Herb's paper bag full of cash lie on the truck seat between us. Every once in a while I would look down at the bag. I don't know why, I guess just because I had never had $100,000 on my truck seat before.

Herb stared out the front windshield while biting the shit out of his fingernails.

"Hungry, Herb?" I asked.

"No. Why?"

"Because you haven't stopped eating your fingers since we got on the road."

"Sorry, I'm just so nervous. I hope she's okay. I can't wait to see her."

"Relax."

"You think everything is going to turn out okay?"

"I have no idea, Herb," I told him. "I think we should have got Tommy Franklin in on this."

"But they would have killed her."

I couldn't argue with that ... again. *What else could we talk about for an hour and a half?* I wondered. *Oh yeah.* "So Bambi used to be a porn star?"

Herb looked at me out of the corner of his eye and then back at the road ahead. "Adult film star," he corrected.

"Yeah, that's what I meant. So you knew about that?"

"Of course I did, Cole. That's how I met her. We met on the set, when I was still married to my first wife."

"The first wife that disappeared."

"Yes."

"Wait. What? Met her on the set? Were you a porn star too, Herb?"

"No. Don't be ridiculous. I was an investor, and I was part owner in the production company that held Bambi's contract. That's how I made my money, Cole. When I sold my share of the company, I bought the Jetty Lounge with some of the money."

"*Some* of the money? How much did you get for your share of the company?"

"Seven million."

"Nice," was all I could think to say. "So, I have to ask, what exactly happened with your first wife?"

"She went for a walk on the beach and never came home."

"I don't understand."

"Jane suffered from severe bouts of depression. As long as she was on her medication, she was fine. When she was fine, she thought she didn't need her medication. I would plead with her to stay on her meds, but she would stop, and then after a few months, she was right back where she started. There were two suicide attempts ... pills both times. One day, when she was at her worst, she decided to go for a walk on the beach. I asked her if she wanted me to come with her. She said no, that she wouldn't be long. She kissed me goodbye, told me she loved me, and I never saw her again."

"I'm sorry, Herb." I said. For the first time since Herb asked for my help, I was actually starting to believe him. Maybe he didn't have anything to do with Bambi's disappearance.

"Is there anything else you want to know?" Herb asked.

"Bambi was arrested when she was a kid; the records are sealed. Do you know what that was all about?"

"Like I told Detective Franklin, I don't know anything about that."

As we drove along we talked some more. Herb asked me about my family. I talked about my ex-wife, and my divorce. I told him a little bit about my children. I touched on Angel and her struggle with addiction, without getting into too much detail. Herb spoke more about Bambi. By the time we arrived in Melbourne, I knew more about Herb and Bambi Bean than I knew about people I had known for years.

We got to the Melbourne Square Mall at ten minutes to twelve. I pulled into the entrance between Outback Steakhouse and Smokey Bones Grill. Kelly drove up the street a little farther and hung a right onto Evans Road. He entered the mall parking lot from the west.

I was making my way up the second row of cars when Herb pointed. "There's her car!" he shouted. "There's Bambi's car!"

I whipped into a spot directly across from her navy-blue Audi.

Herb took hold of the door handle and started to get out.

I grabbed his arm. "Wait."

"Wait for what?"

"Just wait." I opened my door and got out. I left the door open, walked out into the aisle, and looked around. I returned to the truck and dialed Kelly's number.

"Yeah?" Kelly answered. He was driving up and down each aisle, acting as though he was searching out that one perfect parking spot.

"See anything … or anyone?" I asked.

"Nothing so far."

Herb reached into his pocket for his spare set of Bambi's keys. "Should I put the money in the car, Cole?" he asked.

"Hold on," I replied. I reached inside my flannel shirt and adjusted my holster.

"Hey, I got something," Kelly said.

I watched his truck patrolling two aisles over from us. "What do you got?"

"There's a guy," Kelly said, "standing just inside the door at Dick's; he's on his cell phone and he's staring out into the parking lot. He's got on denim shorts and a red T-shirt."

I turned my head toward the store like I was looking around. My head continued to turn, but my eyes stopped on the guy in his late forties. He was definitely staring at Bambi's car.

"Stay on the line," I said, "and keep an eye on him." I turned to Herb. "Take the money to the car and put it in the back seat, lock the door, and come back. Don't look around."

Herb quickly jumped out of the truck and ran to Bambi's car. I watched as he unlocked the door and placed the bag on the seat. He ran back to the truck as quickly as he could and got back in. "Let's go," he ordered. "Let's go get my wife."

I climbed back into the truck and started it. I put the cell on speaker and balanced it on my knee. "Kelly?"

"Yeah?"

"Herb and I are heading to the pickup spot."

"Roger that."

"Keep an eye on our guy and the car. When he leaves, follow him. Don't confront him. Just see where he goes."

"You got it."

"And be careful, pal."

"That's just what a chick would say."

*****

Twenty-five minutes later I was making a right onto Ranch Road; Herb was really going to town on his fingernails. He rocked back and forth in anticipation. A few times I even heard him whisper, "Please be there" and "Please be okay."

Ranch Road ran parallel with, and to the east of, I-95, with a distance of a little less than a mile of wooded land separating them. About a mile in we passed a farm on the right, and a couple of houses on the left. After that it was nothing but loblolly pines, bald cypress, and oak trees on our left and farm fields on our right. At around the two-mile point the blacktop ended and we were traveling down a one-lane dirt road. The truck tires kicked up the dry dust as we drove and when I looked in the rearview mirror I could see nothing but a dense brown cloud.

We veered left and the fields ended. There were now trees on both sides of us. The end of the road was in sight. I slowed my truck and looked over at Herb. He could hardly contain himself. I knew it was part fear and part excitement. I stopped and put the truck in park.

"We'll walk the rest of the way," I said.

Herb was out of the truck before I could finish my sentence. He was running toward the clearing at the end of the road.

"Slow down, Herb," I said, and jogged to catch up with him.

We saw her at the same time.

"Oh my God!" Herb hollered. "No! No!"

The lifeless body of a blonde woman floated face down in the shallow, man-made pond.

I reached for my weapon with one hand, and grabbed Herb by the shoulder with the other. He pulled free and sprinted to his wife. When he reached her, he dropped to his knees beside her.

"No! No!" Herb continued to shout.

I stood over him with my weapon drawn scanning the area. "Goddammit," I whispered.

Chapter Seventeen

The worst part of Herb's day was finding his wife floating in a shallow pond. The worst part of my day was calling Tommy Franklin.

It didn't take long before Ranch Road was swarming with cruisers from the Sebastian PD and the Indian River County Sheriff's Department. There was even a helicopter making several passes over the area.

I called Kelly's cell phone before any of the units arrived and got some more bad news; his F-150 was no match for Bambi's Audi. Kelly said he lost the kid within the first twenty minutes, when he made a right onto Ensenada Street off of Caligula Avenue, in Palm Bay. The hundred grand was gone.

After I got off the phone with Kelly I called Tommy. Tommy notified the Palm Bay PD, and they put out an APB on the navy-blue Audi.

"She was strangled somewhere else and her body was dumped there," Tommy told me on Monday, a little after noon. "The medical examiner said she had been dead at least five days."

"So she was probably killed soon after she disappeared," I surmised.

"Looks that way," Tommy agreed. "We figured she was dumped sometime between Thursday night and Friday morning, because the farmer down the road said he was at the pond late Thursday afternoon."

"Any sign of sexual assault?"

"No."

"Any other injuries?"

"A lump and contusion on the left side of her head. The ME said she was hit with something antemortem."

"He know what it was?"

"Something round. Probably three to four inches in diameter."

"He have a theory on what was used to strangle her?"

"Someone's hands," Tommy responded. "The ME said that her hyoid bone was fractured. He says the hit to the head probably knocked her down, and then her attacker straddled her as she lay prostrate."

"Any skin under her fingernails?"

"None. Her car was found this morning abandoned in the Johns River Marsh outside Palm Bay; forensics is going through it now." Tommy slid his empty soda glass toward me.

"You want another one?" I asked.

"No. I better get going."

"Sorry about not giving you a heads-up on the call from the abductor."

"Well, you can't help being an asshole. Statistics show there's always a better chance of getting them back when the police are involved. You know that, Cole" Tommy slid off his stool, and gave me a grin.

"Yeah, but she was dead way before Herb even got the call," I reminded him.

"Yeah, but we know how statistics work; they won't show that."

"No, they won't."

"How's your buddy Herb doing?"

"He's not my buddy, and I haven't seen him since I dropped him off at his place late Friday night. But I would imagine he's not doing that great."

"Yeah," Tommy said on his way out the door, "a hundred grand is a lot of money to lose."

I just shook my head. *What a prick*, I thought. I dumped the ice out of Tommy's glass and went to the kitchen.

"Norma?" I said.

Norma was making salads for the dinner crowd. "Yeah?" she asked.

"I have to run to Kelly Morgan's house and give him a ride to the neurologist."

"Okey-dokey," she replied. "Where's Emily?'

"She's out back on a smoke break."

"Tell her to get in here and finish these salads, and I'll jump behind the bar."

"You got it," I said.

When I walked back through the bar, Frank and Poco were seated on their usual stools. "Hey guys," I said.

"Hey, boss man," Frank replied. They had both started calling me boss or boss man, I guess because they heard Leon say it so often.

"What brings you in on a Monday?"

"My girl says I need to be more spontaneous," Poco replied.

"Not showing up for your date the other night wasn't spontaneous enough for her?" I asked.

"You just can't please some women," said Poco.

"I'll be right with you," I said.

"Take your time," Frank said. "We wouldn't want to interrupt you with a little business."

I pushed open the door that led to the picnic tables. "Emily?"

"Yeah?" she asked. She was sitting on one of the picnic tables with her ankles crossed and her legs stretched out in front of her. She was leaning back against the table.

"Norma needs you in the kitchen."

"Yup," she replied. She took one last long drag on her cigarette and flicked what remained into the sand.

I turned and went back inside, letting the door close behind me. "What can I get you gentlemen?" I asked.

"The usual," Frank said.

I grabbed two LandSharks out of the cooler behind me, popped the tops, and set one in front of each man. "There you go."

Frank laid a fifty on the bar, and Poco tossed up a twenty.

"Take 'em both out of here," Poco said, sliding the twenty forward with his index finger, so I did.

Norma walked out of the kitchen and toward the bar.

"Well, gentlemen," I said, "I'd like to hang around and visit, but I got shit to do."

"That's okay," Frank said. "We'd much rather look at Norma than you."

I went out the door and jogged across Jetty Park to my truck. The whole way I was wondering if Frank really would rather look at Norma than me.

Chapter Eighteen

Everything at the neurologist went just as well as Kelly had hoped it would. She cleared him to drive, and even told him he could go back to work in two weeks, instead of five. He was ready to celebrate, so we went directly from the doctor's office to the Breakwater. When we got there, Allison was behind the bar, and Norma and Emily were waiting tables. For a Monday afternoon, it was pretty busy.

Frank and Poco were still at the bar, and Melvin was on *his* stool as well. Spence sat between Frank and Melvin eating a cheeseburger and drinking a Coke.

I slipped in behind the bar with Allison, and Kelly grabbed one of the empty stools. I poured Kelly a Jack and Coke, and grabbed a Bud Light for myself.

"Day off, Spence?" I asked.

"Yes, sir," he replied. "First day off in nine days."

"I got the day off too," Melvin joked. He raised his glass in the air and then brought it to his lips for a sip.

"Me too," said Kelly.

Frank threw a thumb in Poco's direction. "And this guy's been on the dole four six months. Am I the only one at this bar who works?"

Everyone laughed.

"Yeah, workin's fer losers," said Poco. He raised his glass, and everyone followed suit. "Here's to doin' nothin'."

"Here! Here!" everyone shouted.

Spence took another bite of his burger, chewed, and swallowed. Spence was not a guy who would talk with his mouth full. "Cole, did you hear they found Herb's Audi up in Palm Bay?"

"Yeah, Tommy was in here earlier. He was telling me about it."

"He tell you a judge opened the wife's sealed arrest record from when she was a kid?"

"No, he didn't."

"The arrest was for a DUI, driving without a license, and assault. The judge decided to open the file after Tommy brought him Bambi's death certificate."

"Does Tommy think it has anything to do with her murder?" I asked.

"He said no, but he's going to look into it any way, since he has nothing else to go on."

Around five Tommy Franklin and Dan Kind walked through the door. The bar was full, so Tommy motioned for me to follow him out the side door. Allison had already finished her shift and was sitting with Spence, but I asked her to jump back behind the bar.

"What's up Tommy?" I said. He and Kind were seated on opposite sides of one of the picnic tables. I sat down next to Kind.

"CSU lifted prints off the steering wheel and driver's side door of Bambi's Audi, and matched them to a guy by the name of Bart Renfroe," Tommy said. He slid a 5x7 photograph of a dark-haired man who appeared to be in his late forties in front of me. "Look familiar?"

"Doesn't ring a bell," I said.

"Worked as a jack of all trades," Kind said. "Roofing, siding, flooring … a little bit of everything."

"Got a record?" I asked.

"Of course," Tommy said. "Mostly small stuff: breaking and entering, shoplifting. Nothing violent."

"Any connection to Herb's wife?" I asked.

"Not that we can find," said Kind. "We questioned Herb about it and he said he never heard of the guy."

"You put out an APB on him?" I asked.

"No need," Tommy said. "We already found him."

"What's he saying?"

"Nothing. We found him lying dead on his living room floor, a gunshot to his abdomen and another one to his temple. We haven't got anything back from ballistics yet."

"Spence said they opened Bambi's old arrest record," I said. "Anything?"

"It was a dead end," Kind replied.

"She was Veronica Morton back then," Tommy reminded me. "She got into an altercation with her then-boyfriend and then sped off in *his* car, drunk. The boyfriend, a kid by the name of Stuart Goble, called the police and Veronica was picked up. They charged her with a DUI and operating a motor vehicle without a license."

"Spence said there was something about an assault?" I asked.

Tommy nodded yes. "The report said when Veronica's—that is Bambi's—boyfriend came to pick up his vehicle at the station, he had a fat lip and a black eye. They also noticed Veronica's knuckles were bruised. He was asked if he wanted to press charges, but he declined."

"Probably didn't want his friends to know he got his ass kicked by a girl," said Kind.

"Probably," I agreed. "So, what's next?"

"Well, we're off duty, so next I think I'll have a good stiff drink," Tommy said.

"Sounds good to me," Kind agreed.

I picked up the photograph of Bart Renfroe. "Can I hang on to this, Tommy?" I asked.

"What for?"

"I'll probably stop over to Herb's tomorrow and see how he's doing. I want to take the photograph with me."

"What are you thinking?" Tommy asked.

"Nothing," I said. "I just think Herb let's his guard down a little around me."

Tommy shrugged. "Whatever. Keep it."

I dropped the photo into the side pocket of my cargo shorts.

The three of us went back inside. A few bar stools had freed up, one being Melvin's. Tommy and Kind joined the group and I made them each a drink.

"Melvin take off?" I asked. "Or is he in the shitter?"

"He left," Spence said. He winced slightly at my salty language, like he always did.

"Said he had a date," Poco added.

"Probably with his hand," Kelly deadpanned.

*****

Spence and Allison took off around six. Tommy and Kind left around seven, and Frank and Poco left soon after. The dinner crowd had dwindled down to only one table.

"Norma, can you watch the bar?" I asked. "I have to run Kelly home. I won't be long."

"Yup," she said, and waved on her way through to the kitchen.

Kelly and I walked to my truck. I backed out of my parking spot and headed down Seaway Drive. As we drove by Herb's place I noticed the building was dark, and the "closed until further notice" sign was still hanging in the window.

"That buddy of yours still work at Home Depot?" I asked.

"Which one?" Kelly asked. "I know about four or five people who work there."

"His name was Jim ... or John, or something."

"There's a Jim and a John I know who work there."

"Whichever, I don't care. Can you run over there with me tomorrow morning?"

"Sure. What are you building?"

"Nothing. I just want to ask a few questions."

"This about Herb Bean?"

"Yes."

"You supposed to be doing this?"

"No one told me not to."

"What time in the morning?"

"I'll pick you up and take you to breakfast around nine, then we'll shoot over to Home Depot."

"Sounds good."

At that point Kelly changed the subject, and all he talked about for the rest of the ride, was taking a ride over to Fellsmeer and having a little talk with Chief Clyde Reese. I, smiled, and even nodded my head a few times, just to humor him. The truth was, the more he talked about it the more I came to realize that it was probably a bad idea. Sure, I wanted to get even with that prick for what he helped his kid and his friends do to Kelly, but I also didn't want to see me or Kelly wind up in jail for it.

I listened to him yammer on and on right up until we turned the corner onto his street; that's when we saw all the flashing lights. I slowed down and pulled to the curb about two houses up from Kelly's and shut off my engine.

"What the hell is going on here?" Kelly asked.

"I don't know," I said.

We both got out of the truck and walked the rest of the way. When we arrived at the yellow caution tape that ran from tree to tree to mailbox post around Kelly's neighbor's house, a uniformed officer stopped us.

"Y'all gotta stay behind the tape," the officer said.

I reached for my wallet and showed my gold shield. Sure, it now said "retired" across the badge, but it still got me into places where civilians weren't allowed.

"What happened?" I asked.

"You live on this street?" the officer asked.

"No." I nodded my head in Kelly's direction. "My buddy here lives next door."

"Lady beat her husband to death with an ashtray," said the officer.

"Holy shit!" Kelly blurted out.

"Who's the detective on the scene?" I asked.

"Rodriguez."

"You know him?" Kelly asked.

"No," I said.

"He just transferred here from Orlando," said the officer. "Worked in internal affairs up there I guess."

I craned my neck to watch as two paramedics wheeled the husband out in a body bag. "Well, if you need anything, we'll be in the house," I remarked to the cop, he tipped his cap politely. I turned and started up Kelly's driveway. "I guess we should have called the cops the other day," I whispered. "It may have embarrassed the guy, but at least he might still be alive."

"I'd rather be dead," Kelly whispered back.

Chapter Nineteen

When I got back to the Breakwater, Angel was sitting on one of the barstools. Norma was standing behind the bar. Angel was grinning big and even laughing as Norma spoke. Angel always laughed and smiled when she was using. It was her game. She reminded me of a used car salesman or a lawyer. Smile, laugh, and be everyone's friend, that way maybe one of them would give you a few bucks when you worked it into a conversation. It sure as hell didn't fool me, and I know it didn't fool Norma either, but the addict always thinks they're in control.

"Hey, kid," I said.

"Hi, Daddy," Angel replied. She gave me a huge smile. Those teeth were still perfect, even after all the years of abuse.

I walked over to her and gave her a hug. She felt thin and frail. She was wearing too much perfume to mask the odor of whatever it was she didn't want me to notice. "Leon making you something to eat?" I asked.

"Yes. He's making me a chicken quesadilla and some French fries."

Norma got out from behind the bar. She squeezed my shoulder as she walked behind me. It was her way of saying, "Hang in there."

"I haven't seen you in a while," I said.

"I've been pretty busy," Angel replied. She kept Norma in her peripheral, and when she knew she was out of earshot she focused her eyes back on me. The smile left her face, and it was replaced by something almost evil. "Well, have you thought about what I said?"

"What you said?" I questioned.

"About money."

"What about money?"

Angel looked around the room. "I know you have more money than you let on. Donnie says anyone who owns a bar on the beach like this is loaded."

"I'm not going to discuss my financial situation with you," I told her. "And who's Donny?"

"He's my boyfriend," Angel replied. "He says you should be helping me out. A good father wouldn't cut me out. He says you should be giving me money."

"First of all, I didn't cut you out, you cut yourself out. Second, if *Donny* was a good boyfriend he would have a job, and he would be helping you out."

"What makes you think he don't have a job?"

"Just a guess."

"He had a job, but his boss was always riding his ass, so he quit."

"Oh, I see, so it was his boss's fault. I would imagine every job Donny's ever lost was someone else's fault. He sounds like a girl I know."

"Fuck you," Angel shot back. She was growing more agitated. I could tell it had been awhile since she had used. "Sorry I'm not perfect like your little Allison."

"I never said she was perfect."

"You and Mom always liked her better."

"No … we didn't."

"You never let *me* work here."

"Get clean and stay clean, and maybe someday you can work here."

"Follow your rules."

"They're most people's rules."

Angel dug at a scab on her arm and it started to bleed. I reached over and grabbed a napkin from the dispenser. I laid it on the bar in front of her. "Here," I said. "Angel, I love you, so does your mother, CJ, and Allison. Any of the problems you have, you've created for yourself. We've tried to help you time and time again. If you're hungry, I'll feed you. If you need clothing, I'll buy you something to wear, but I'm not giving you a dime."

"You self-righteous bastard. You think I'm so horrible. Well let me tell you something: I've never murdered anyone."

I didn't reply. I just stood with my hands on the bar. I sure as hell wasn't about to admit to killing Ted Hale. Like most addicts, Angel was good at manipulating a situation and getting what she wanted; she was a smart kid. For all I know she had her cell phone in her pocket and was recording our conversation.

"Nothing?" Angel said. "You have nothing to say?"

"What do you want me to say?"

"I want you to admit that you killed Ted. I want you to admit that you're not perfect."

"I have no idea what you're talking about."

"I was at your apartment that night, sleeping in the guest room. Remember? I saw you leave with your gun. I saw you. The next day we found out Ted had been murdered. I know you did it."

"Like I said, I have no idea what you're talking about."

Leon walked out of the bar and placed Angel's plate in front of her. "Here you go, little princess," he said. "Real crispy, just like you like it."

With both hands Angel shoved the plate across the bar; it shattered on the floor next to my feet. "Keep your damn food!" she screamed.

Leon stepped back.

Angel leaned in close to me and said, "Donny says if you don't give us five grand, we go to the cops. You have three days."

Angel hopped off her barstool with over-exaggerated confidence and walked out the door.

"Boss," Leon asked, "is every—"

"Everything is fine, Leon," I said. "Kids."

I pulled my cell phone out of my pocket and started to dial. I stopped and tossed it on the bar, deciding instead to use the landline. I dialed.

"Fort Pierce Police Department," a woman answered. "How may I direct your call?"

"Hello," I said. "My name is Cole Ballinger, I'm a retired Fort Pierce Police officer ... a .357 Smith and Wesson revolver ... I don't know, it could have been taken anytime in the last year. The box sits in the bottom drawer of my desk, and I haven't even looked in there in quite a while ... yes, I'll hold, thank you."

Leon cocked his head. "Is there something I should know, boss?"

I knew there were only six people who would know I was lying about the missing gun: Two of them were dead, three of them were in jail, and Leon. I was positive I could trust Leon. I put my hand over the mouthpiece and whispered, "I'll explain everything after I get off the phone, but first, go grab a hammer."

Chapter Twenty

I picked up Kelly at his place a little after nine the following morning, a Tuesday. We ate breakfast at Dave's Diner and then headed for Home Depot. Kelly called his buddy, Jim, before I arrived to make sure he was working. He was, and so was his other buddy, John.

Kelly tried to bring up Fellsmere again on the way over, but like Barney Fife would say, I nipped it in the bud.

"I need to pick up a few things while we're here," Kelly said as we pulled into the parking lot.

"For what?" I asked. "This wasn't supposed to be a shopping trip."

"Well you never told me what type of trip it was."

"I just want to ask around about Bart Renfroe. I figured this was as good a place as any to start."

"You should have just said so, then. Who the hell is Bart Renfroe?"

"He's the guy you were supposed to follow. The guy who you lost … along with Herb's hundred grand."

"Oh. How did you find out his name?"

"Tommy Franklin told me. They found his prints in Bambi's car."

"Did they arrest him?"

"No. They found him dead in his home when they arrived. He had been shot twice."

"What does he have to do with Home Depot?"

"He's a contractor, and I figure this is the closest Home Depot to his place, and also Herb Bean's house."

I pulled into a parking spot and shut off the engine. We got out and walked toward the buildings contractor entrance. "What is it you need to buy while we're here?" I asked.

"Some molding for around my sliding glass door. The door you threw my patio chair through."

"You mean the one I smashed so I could get inside your house and save your life?"

"Whatever."

"Yeah, whatever. You're welcome. Besides, I thought the contractor already fixed that door."

We walked through the automatic sliding door and continued on to the rear of the store.

"He just put in the new door. I told him I would do the moldings and painting. I didn't want to spend that much."

"Why, didn't your home owners insurance cover it?"

"I have a five thousand dollar deductible."

"Five thousand bucks?" I asked. "Isn't that kinda high?"

"Well, in my wildest dreams I never thought one of my friends would throw a chair though my sliding glass door."

"Expect the unexpected."

"I lowered my deductible to five hundred after that. But you watch, with my luck nothing will ever happen again."

"Yeah, with your luck."

Jim Meadows worked in the kitchen cabinets department. When we got there, he was standing next to an old blue-haired lady. He was rattling off his sales spiel and pointing at various cabinets. The blue-hair nodded her head politely, feigning interest.

"Hey, John," Kelly said.

"Hey, what's up, Morgan?" John shot back.

"Got a couple questions for you."

He put up his index finger. "Hold on. As soon as I'm done with this lady."

"Yup," Kelly replied.

While we waited, I looked at the nearby cabinets. I opened and shut a few doors and pulled on a couple drawers.

"Thinking about putting in a new kitchen?" Kelly asked.

"I live in an apartment," I responded.

"Oh yeah."

"When I want a new kitchen I'll move."

"What can I do for you guys?" John asked.

I turned around. The blue hair was gone.

"We didn't ruin a sale for you, did we, John?" Kelly stuck out his hand and they shook.

"Nah. That old bag wasn't gonna buy anything," John replied.

"John, this is a friend of mine, Cole Ballinger. Cole, John Meadows."

"Oh yeah, the retired cop who owns the bar," John said. "Kelly talks about you all the time."

"Yeah, he's in love with me," I joked.

John laughed. "How come you never play poker with us guys?"

I looked at Kelly. "I don't know why."

"You should some night. It's an excuse to get out of the house."

"Maybe I will."

"John," Kelly said, "Cole was wondering if he could ask you a few questions."

"Sure. What's up?"

I reached in my pocket for the photograph of Bart Renfroe. "You know this guy?" I asked.

John leaned into the picture. "Yeah, yeah, that's Bart. Bart … Renfield, or something."

"Renfore," I said.

"Yeah, Renfroe. He's a local contractor."

"Can you tell me if he was in here last Saturday night or Sunday?"

"Hmm. He could have been, I guess. I'm not sure."

"I'm thinking he might have bought some carpeting," I said.

John looked at Kelly. "Well, why don't we go ask Jim; he works in flooring. If he was here last weekend, maybe he remembers."

Kelly and I followed John down about eight aisles to the flooring department. A guy in his early fifties, medium build with brown hair, was on one knee pulling tack strip out of one bin and sliding it into another.

"Jim," John called out.

Jim rose up and hit his head on the steel shelf above him. "Son of a bitch!" he swore. "What do you want?" He stood up and turned around, rubbing the back of his head.

"Were you on last Sunday?" John asked.

"Yeah." He thought for a second. "Open to four."

"You know Bart Renfroe, right?"

"Yeah. Why? He in trouble?"

"Do you remember if he was in here last Sunday?" I asked.

"He was. He came in early and bought around two hundred square feet of carpeting."

"What color?"

Jim pointed at the gigantic floor to ceiling carpet rack. "Right there. The Stainmaster TruSoft."

I looked behind me. "The beige one?"

"Yeah. I cut it for him myself."

"Thanks, Jim," I said. "Come on, Kelly." I turned and hurried down the aisle.

"What about my molding?" Kelly called out.

"We'll get it tomorrow."

Kelly hurried to catch up with me. "What's the matter?"

"I'm not sure," I said. "I'm going to drop you back at your house. There's somewhere I have to be."

"Do you need any help?"

"No," I said. "I got it covered."

Chapter Twenty-One

I knocked on Herb Bean's door a little before noon on Tuesday. When he opened the door, he was glad to see me, or maybe not. Herb was good at hiding his true feelings.

"Cole! Hey, how's it going?" Herb stood in the doorway. He was still in his pajamas, a robe, and house slippers.

"Good, Herb."

"What brings you out here?" He showed some excitement.

"I just wanted to check up on you. Make sure you were doing okay."

The excitement of my unexpected arrival was replaced by the somber face of a man who had just lost the love of his life. "Come on in," he said, and pulled the door open.

I walked in and Herb shut the door behind me. He led me to the living room. The television was on and a half-empty mug of coffee set on the coffee table; next to it was the daily paper. "I was just having a cup of coffee, Cole. Would you like one?"

"Sure, Herb. Thanks."

"Comin' right up." He turned and walked down the hall toward the kitchen.

I turned and looked at the television. Oddly enough, it was tuned to an old episode of *Forensic Files*.

"It's cold in here, Herb," I called out.

Herb shouted back from the kitchen, "Yeah, Bambi never liked the air conditioning turned up. She was always cold."

She's a lot colder now, I thought. "Watching *Forensic Files* again, I see."

Herb returned with my coffee and handed me the mug. "Black, right?" he said. "No sugar."

"That's right. You've got a good memory, Herb."

He glanced over at the TV. "One of my favorite shows," he said. "Sit down. Take a load off."

Herb sat on the couch, and I took a seat in a chair adjacent to the couch. I blew into my mug and then took a sip. "What's that, pumpkin spice?" I asked.

"Yes it is," Herb replied. "Bambi never liked flavored coffees."

"Seems like Bambi never liked a lot of things," I commented.

"What do you mean?"

"Well, she didn't like the air conditioner on, she didn't like flavored coffee, and you told me the first day I was here that she didn't like cleaning. It must be nice to do what you want now."

"I wouldn't say nice—I mean, under the circumstances and all." Herb continued to stare at the television. Two detectives had a black man in the interrogation room. He was claiming to know nothing about the crime he was being accused of. Herb grinned and snorted. "You ever notice, Cole, the detectives rarely actually catch the guy on their own."

"What do you mean, Herb?"

"The cops in this show ... they rarely have enough evidence to convict the suspect. The guy usually ends up confessing after hours of interrogation. I always wonder why the guy doesn't lawyer up the minute he's accused. Well, you know, you used to be a cop."

I nodded my head. "A lot of it does come down to the interrogation."

"I don't think I would be that stupid."

"You don't?"

"No. I don't."

"Let's give it a try, Herb."

Herb sipped his coffee. "Okay."

"I think you killed Bambi," I said.

"You do?" His facial expression didn't change. I anticipated some kind of surprise.

"Yes, I do."

"And what makes you think that?"

"Well, for starters, I think Bambi was a bitch."

"Cole, that's my wife you're talking about ... God rest her soul."

"I think she was mean. I think she had anger issues, and I think she may have even slapped you around a little bit. A little guy like you, you probably couldn't even defend yourself. I think if the house wasn't clean, you caught hell about it. I think if it was too cold in here, she bitched at you about it. I think all you wanted was a little flavored coffee, but she denied it to you." I added pointedly, "I bet she denied you lots of things."

"Go on," Herb said.

"I think the two of you got in an argument last Saturday. It got a little worse than usual. You hit her in the head with a bottle of wine, causing the gash in her head. That's what caused the blood stain on the carpet."

"It wasn't blood, Cole. The stain was red wine. The lab tested it."

"Oh I'm not talking about the rug that's there now. I'm talking about the rug that was there *before* Bart Renfroe bought the new rug on Sunday morning at Home Depot and installed it for you."

Herb pretended to stay calm. He was pretty good at pretending, but his eyes told a different story.

"After Renfroe installed the new carpet, you poured half a bottle of red wine right on top of where the bloodstain was because you knew they would cut out that section of carpet and test it. If it tested negative for blood, that would be enough for them. You knew they wouldn't test the plywood subfloor underneath. But, Herb, I'm guessing if someone sprayed a little bit of Luminol on that plywood, it would turn blue. I don't have to explain Luminol to you, do I, Herb? After all, you watch a lot of *Forensic Files*."

"I know what Luminol is."

"After the carpet was done, you and Renfroe hatched the plan to dump Bambi at the pond. The only reason you didn't want us to drive down I-95 is because you wanted me to believe there was someone there watching the pond. Then you double-crossed Renfroe, killed him, and took back your hundred grand. I bet if we went into your safe right now, we would find that money right back in there safe and sound."

"There's a lot of money in there, sure" Herb said. "That doesn't prove anything."

"There's a lot of money, Herb. But only a few hundred dollar bills have the corners torn off."

"Corners torn off?"

"When you weren't looking I tore the corners off of about six bills."

"You son of a bitch," Herb said with a grin. "I guess you got me."

"I thought you were too smart to confess?"

"It's only you, and you're not a cop anymore."

"But I'll be a witness."

"No," Herb said, as he pulled the snub-nosed revolver out of his robe pocket. "You'll be dead."

"You'll have to buy a new chair," I said. "There'll be blood all over this one."

"I can afford a new chair," he replied. "Bambi had some life insurance."

"Is that why you did it, Herb—the money?"

"No. I have plenty of my own money. You were right; it was just because she was a bitch."

Herb raised his weapon, and I shoved my chair over backwards. He fired, hitting me in the left shoulder.

I reached into the large side pocket of my cargo shorts and grabbed my .38.

Herb fired again, hitting a wooden brace on the bottom of the chair. He fired a third time, hitting the sheetrock behind me.

I rose up and shot twice, striking him once in the stomach and once in the arm. He dropped the weapon and stumbled back onto the couch. It was then I heard the sirens. I knew Tommy was on his way; I had called him from Herb's driveway.

I kept my gun trained on Herb's torso as I walked toward him. "I bet the bullets they pulled out of old Bart Renfroe match that .22 of yours, Herb."

Herb was holding his stomach wound. "I want my lawyer," he groaned. "I want my lawyer."

"I bet you do," I replied. "Keep pressure on that, buddy."

Chapter Twenty-Two

"You still got that sling on?" asked Tommy Franklin. "It's been four days for chrissakes."

I was standing behind the bar at the Breakwater. The lunch crowd had filed out and the dinner crowd hadn't arrived. "I got shot, ya bastard."

"I know, but it was just a .22."

"A .22 magnum," I corrected.

Tommy climbed onto one of the barstools. "That's like saying, 'It was a BB gun *magnum*.'"

"He killed someone with that same gun a couple days earlier," I argued. "You're a dick."

"You're a pussy."

"What'll you have?"

"Jack and Coke."

I grabbed a glass and filled it with ice. "So, did old Herb spill his guts in interrogation?"

"He hasn't admitted to a damn thing. His lawyer is trying to get him a plea deal."

"What kind of deal?"

"I don't know. Probably life without parole, instead of the death penalty. It's in the DA's hands now."

"Life's better than death, I guess. Maybe they'll even let him watch *Forensic Files* on the inside."

Tommy laughed. "Yeah, maybe."

I slid his drink across the bar to him. He took a big gulp.

The front door opened and in walked two men. I knew they were detectives the second they entered. They had that look. The look I once had, or maybe still do. One was tall and thin. He had black hair slicked back to his scalp, and wore Rayban Wayfarers. He didn't take off his sunglasses when he entered the room. The other guy was about two inches shorter and thirty pounds heavier. He had dark hair as well, but wore it short—buzzed on the sides and back and finger length on top. He removed his aviators.

Tommy looked over; he looked a little confused. "Hey, Rodriguez."

"Franklin," Rodriguez replied.

"What brings you in here?"

Rodriguez didn't answer him. "You Cole Ballinger?" he asked.

"I am," I replied.

"You know why we're here?"

"I don't even know who you are."

"I'm Detective Amelio Rodriguez, and this is Detective Marcus Wagner. We're with the Fort Pierce Police Department."

"It's nice to meet you," I said. "What can I do for you?"

"We got a complaint," said Wagner.

"About the noise?" I asked.

"No," Rodriguez replied. "About the murder."

"What murder would that be?"

"The murder of one Ted Hale," said Rodriguez.

"Just one?" I asked. "How many Ted Hales are there?"

Neither Rodriguez nor Wagner thought I was funny. Thankfully, Tommy chuckled or I would have thought I was losing it.

"Did you know Ted Hale?"

"I knew *a* Ted Hale. He used to date my daughter."

"And do you know what happened to him?"

"He died," I said.

"Do you know anything about that?" Wagner asked.

"I know that when your heart stops pumping blood to your brain it causes—"

"Listen, asshole—"

"Rodriguez!" Tommy shouted.

"I got this!" Rodriguez shouted back, putting up a hand. "We got a call last night. The caller is accusing you of the murder of Ted Hale. The caller says they confronted you about the murder on Saturday night. Coincidentally, it's the same night you called and reported a stolen firearm."

"Wow, that is a coincidence," I said. Herb Bean's words echoed in my head. *The detectives rarely actually catch the guy on their own.*

"Rodriguez," Tommy said. "Cole used to be a cop."

"I know," Rodriguez said.

"Who's this mystery caller?" I asked.

"It was an anonymous call," Wagner replied.

"Well, let me know when it's not," I said. "And in the meantime, can I offer you gentlemen a drink?"

Wagner slid his aviators back on and turned toward the door. "Maybe another time."

Rodriguez gave Tommy a look. "I don't drink on duty," he said.

"I'm off duty, asshole," Tommy said.

Rodriguez looked from Tommy to me. "I'm *always* on duty," he said, and followed his partner out the door.

"Wow," I said. "Somebody spent their childhood watching way too many cop shows."

Tommy didn't laugh. "Please tell me you didn't have anything to do with that piece of shit's death."

"Okay. I didn't have anything to do with that piece of shit's death."

"Thank you."

"You're welcome."

The End

Coming Soon:

Local Hero

A Dunquin Cove Story

ALSO BY RODNEY RIESEL

From the Tales of Dan Coast Series

Sleeping Dogs Lie
Ocean Floors
The Coast of Christmas Past
Ship of Fools
Double Trouble
Most Likely to Die
Deadly Moves
On the Wagon
No Enemies Here

Jake Stellar Series

North Murder Beach
Beach Shoot
When Death Returns
The Obedience of Fools
Dead in the Water
Excited About Nothing

The Dunquin Cove Series

The Man in Room Number Four
Return to Dunquin Cove
Local Hero

Sunrise City Series
Sunrise City
Sunrise City 2: From Bad to Worse
Never Strikes Twice

Fernandina Beach Mysteries
Maintenance Required
High Maintenance

From Here to There: A Collection of Short Stories